New Desires
Modern Short Stories

By
'Maha Mahopadhyaya'
B. S. RAMULU
Social Philosopher
BC Commission First Chairman,
Telangana State.

ALL RIGHTS RESERVED

All rights reserved. No part of this publication may be reproduced, stored in or introduced into a retrieval system, or transmitted, in any form by any means may it be electronically, mechanical, optical, chemical, manual, photocopying, or recording without prior written permission of the Publisher/ Author.

New Desires
Modern Short Stories
By
B. S. Ramulu

Ph: +91 8331966987
Copy Right: B. S. Ramulu

Published By: Kasturi Vijayam
Published on: May,2024

ISBN (Paperback): 978-81-969150-1-8

Print On Demand

Ph:0091-9515054998
Email: Kasturivijayam@gmail.com
Book Available
@
Amazon (Worldwide), flipkart

New Desires
Modern Short Stories

FOREWORD

The stories of this book were written recently. There is something special about these stories. They are tales that simply tell how philosophy exists in life. Behind events, there are some reasons. Behind some thoughts, there is a philosophy. Everyone experiences emotions. Everyone thinks philosophically. However, they act according to their needs.

Some people express themselves with emotions they have already framed. Some gestures, memories, and reminders spontaneously emerge in their minds. Some people intentionally try to forget certain memories. Some sweet memories resurface repeatedly.

People live by constantly pursuing desires. When one wish is fulfilled, another sprouts. A wish is like something that doesn't exist within itself. Fulfilling it brings joy. They live happily. Yet, desires do not stop there. Desires are the reason for the development of goals. Buddha said that desires are the cause of suffering. Now, desires have become necessities of life. A person gradually adapts to how things unfold, how he can grow are decided by them...!

However, when goals are accompanied by greed, one may not be able to enjoy the happiness that should come with achieved successes. Such people fall into despair. Someone has to come and tell them and need to acknowledge their achievements. Then they will realize that they too are winners in life and will be happy.

People think that the opportunities they lost in life will never come back. But opportunities do come. One must recognize them and with courage, one must take a step forward. Then a new life begins.

Some believe that their will is their freedom. They think they have decided their own desires. However, their likes and dislikes are often dictated by circumstances and timely situations. Is there selfishness in freedom? Or are they mistaking selfishness for freedom? It's something that doesn't become clear all at once

Before seeing a beautiful object, the thought of buying it does not occur. After seeing it, one feels the desire to purchase it. People grow by observing others. Those who have advanced before inspire others. Before seeing a girl or a boy, there is no opinion about them. Upon seeing them, a feeling arises. Emotions like love and friendship begin to sprout. Thus, human relationships can be formed.

In a life that has passed, there may be some sorrows. Those who learn that there are ways to overcome these sorrows will win in life.

When the occasion is changed, even the rejoicing things in life can become melancholic. How can one overcome that sadness? How can they find new thoughts beyond sorrow? When moods change, life takes on different shades.

Some people love. People can love beyond caste and religion if they are not impure by any means. When people reject love based on caste or impure feelings, what happens? If someone's son or daughter has committed suicide due to unrequited love, what is the result? Parents, friends, and egos sacrifice their lives and is it necessary? But when parents and relatives agree to inter-caste marriages, it is an ideal step forward. Therefore, someone must come forward. Parents should accept it.

Inter-caste marriages have been continuing for centuries. Even ancient literature has examples of such unions. In modern times, parents themselves are taking the initiative to solemnize marriages beyond caste barriers, approving of the relationships their children cherish. Parents seeking inter-caste marriages for their children is an even more progressive step forward.

It takes courage to find someone you love and marry them. It may take some time. When children of a generation that doesn't understand caste have to marry on their own… it's a rare occasion when everyone comes together to form a family.

In Bigg Boss, they live together in one place for months. Only certain situations and scenes are shown on TV. Many relationships are formed during the time they spend there. What happens to those relationships once they return to their lives outside? If one person becomes a star and the other remains where they were, how trivial life seems! Even a successful life may seem superficial if it doesn't fill the emptiness in the heart. How would it be if such unrelated scenes occur in life, and they talk about it...!

The COVID-19 era turned the world upside down and tested human relationships. It was a difficult time for society, limiting people to the idea of surviving on their own. In such tough times, how could millions who could only survive by working as laborers live? What should the students do when schools and hostels are closed? Who should fulfill their needs? What would their sweet memories be like? How painful it must be to celebrate a birthday alone at home, which should be celebrated with everyone? There is a story about what those children might do then.

In a changed village, the mindsets remain unchanged. If the mindsets don't change, is it as if the village hasn't changed? What should be done to change mindsets as if the village has changed? What will they do? One person's sacrifice can inspire another to find happiness. Tragic endings can show society the way to happy endings. Suicides will stop if there is someone who loves them. The call of age should come naturally. We must get closer to naturalness. For that, elders must cooperate and clear doubts.

The victories accomplished materialize great happiness in lives and its inspiration remains. Despite the passage of decades, that joy remains fresh and new. Life itself renews with every moment. The happiness experienced due to the emergence of Telangana is not something easily expressed.

Some economic relationships develop through human connections. However, there are those who consider all human relationships as economic ones. There are many friendships and bonds that exist without the influence of financial ties. These can sometimes be strained amidst financial relationships but will bloom again when needed. Money makes a person run for it, leaving everyone behind. When they fall into a pit, they look back. That's how human relationships flourish again.

In a life that has passed, there may be some sorrows. There are also ways to overcome these sorrows. The heart plays a role in choosing these paths. Past experiences serve as warnings. If one proceeds with courage, success follows. Life goes on happily. If one remains contemplative, life just passes by. Those who move forward with courage, how wonderful their life becomes! Similarly, if one remains contemplative, how that turns out can be seen in another story.

When a person is working towards a goal, he may sometimes feel disheartened. To overcome this despair, the support of close ones is essential. With their help, one can emerge from disappointment. In movements that bring people together to work towards a common cause, hearts open up and love blossoms. It is then that such movements truly unite people and keep them united. These movements foster human relationships, love, and friendship between men and women.

These are the themes discussed in this collection of stories. They are modern tales. These stories depict various aspects, problems, and their solutions in modern life. I chose to portray life in this simple style of sculpture. It is through this that I was able to express ideas briefly, concisely, and philosophically.

In the state of Telangana, there have been many struggles, numerous conflicts, and several phases that needed to be depicted as part of life. Various contradictions, clashes, parental pressures, and situations faced by representatives who sacrificed their positions and roles are portrayed. Due to them, Telangana state experienced a period of stagnation. Along with TRS leaders, even Congress party members resigned, causing further difficulties for the people of Telangana. Several suicides occurred due to urgent circumstances. People contemplate within their own methods. The reason behind contemplating suicide before taking any action is the resignation of Telangana Congress leaders, who chose to resign from their positions. As a result, students, youth, and entrepreneurs have faced numerous challenges, and many initiatives have been undertaken…! Within this context, some angles can be seen in stories like 'OU Campus' and 'The call of the age'.

In the final stages of life, within the subconscious minds of individuals who lie dormant, there exist desires, emotions, love, hopes, and goals. However, there is nothing left to be done. Yet, these continue to inspire the close friends around them. They give meaning to life. In the story 'Preyasi Vasthunna…' (meaning 'Beloved is Coming…'), reflections on life's final stages, conversations, and a new beginning can be found. These stories, set in the context of Telangana's industrial progression, should serve as a source of motivation for contemplating life, achieving new beginnings, and addressing the needs of modern life. Let these narratives guide us toward fresh aspirations and determination.

I express my gratitude to the editors of Namaste Telangana, Sakshi, Vaarta, and Vishalandhra newspapers. I extend my thanks to the editors of Nijam Daily, Bhaisa Devadasu, Navamalliteega monthly magazine, Mayookha (an internet magazine), and Vedagiri Rambabu 'Janmadina Kathalanikalu 'compilation of short stories. These stories are a reflection of life's final stages, contemplations, and new beginnings. They serve as a source of inspiration for contemplating life, achieving fresh starts, and addressing the needs of modern life. Let these narratives guide us toward renewed aspirations and determination.

***

Table of Contents

1.	NEW DESIRES	1
2.	A NEW LIFE	7
3.	MY VILLAGE	18
4.	RELA	22
5.	THE VICTOR	30
6.	A SHATTERED DREAM	38
7.	THE FISH	44
8.	GURUKULAM	49
9.	SHADES	57
10.	THE STRINGS OF HEART	60
11.	OSMANIA UNIVERSITY CAMPUS	72
12.	YOUTHFUL LOVE SPARKS	87
13.	NEW! EVERYTHING IS ENTIRELY NEW!	101
14.	OH, MY DEAR! I AM COMING!	109
15.	MONEY	118
16.	LIBERATION FROM FREEDOM	127

NEW DESIRES

Satyam had no large desires. His new longings often arose in his mind. He wished to pursue Intermediate course after his tenth class. He intended to study degree on completion of Intermediate course.

After degree he thought of studying P.G. course at the University. He yearned for doing Ph.D. only after P.G. After Ph.D. he wanted to become a university professor. After he became a professor, he attempted to attend national and international seminars. He was intent on publishing books only after attending seminars. His longings went on growing gradually.

During boyhood Sathyam aimed at learning cycling. After he learnt cycling, he wanted to buy a bicycle.

Later he longed for going to a village riding a bicycle. Several new desires sprang in his mind when he was in fifth class. He wanted to have a good pen and pencil. He craved for a new notebook, new books, and new dresses. He wished to earn the first place in all games. He aimed at winning praises from his teachers.

Sitting in the last bench he thought of keeping tails behind the shorts of front benchers.

Sathyam thought of getting married after he studied Intermediate course. He was married only after the completion of his graduation. After P.G, he was blessed with children. When his age grew, he wished to have a lovely wife. When he had a pretty wife, he wanted to have a house of his own. He imagined that his wife, Janaki, should pursue education.

He got his wife educated. She took up a job later. Janaki was like a loving sister to Sathyam in many respects.

Sathyam had no anxiety whatsoever.

He had a good job, a lovely wife, a well-built house and earned respect in social circles.

Sathyam was keen on reducing his desires. Eating food is also a desire.

Why do longings arise in the mind?

Why do new desires spring? As water springs in a well, the desires spring in our mind's day by day. Where is the source of our desires?

Sathyam held discussions with Janaki regarding the philosophy of Buddha. He desired to know whether there was sainthood in the philosophy of Buddha. He had school-going children by then. He wanted them to receive good education. They should grow as he grew. The couple discussed why these new longings were arising in the mind. A seed becomes a plant, and a plant becomes a tree. The tree has many seeds. There will be new plants. New longings spring one by one.

Sathyam wanted to be happy with a bicycle when he was a student of Intermediate. After degree he wished to own a wife, a bicycle, a wristwatch, and a radio. All these articles came with the arrival of wife in his life. With his wife came a bicycle, a wristwatch, a radio and a fan. He possessed more things than he craved for. He was satisfied with what he obtained. After Ph.D. He wished to have a scooter. He intended to purchase a scooter with his scholarship. Janaki collected some articles from the house of her parents. The couple bought a scooter.

They travelled on scooter along with their children to various places. They wished to see a film every week. He longed to discuss advantages and disadvantages of films. He set up a film society. They were desirous of showing good films to the people. Ten people together watched good films shown to them. They felt that they would know a lot of things by watching such films.

Janaki's mother worked as a teacher. His brother-in-law was inclined to become a lecturer like Sathyam. Janaki's sister was a wholesale trader. She was eager to achieve growth. Sathyam's sister, Shravya, left for America with her husband. She was enthusiastic to be an employee. Thus, they would be happy. Sathyam had a penchant for visiting America. He went there to attend International Seminars twice.

With the intention of watching Japan,

he went there to attend two seminars.

Sathyam hoped to buy and read good books. He nurtured a yearning to set up his own library at home. He bought new books for the library. He did not stop there. He thought of reading them intently. He did not remain silent after going through the books. He analyzed those books. He published his analyses in the form of a book. He did not stay silent after the publication of book. He was bent on writing a review. He published a new book thereafter. Many people showered praises on him. His students grew up. They became teachers. They were moulded as lecturers. They met him by chance.

They would prostrate before him. They would say that he was their *guru*. His heart would overflow with boundless joy. His heart would be rejoiced.

Sathyam's neighbours earned good life. He experienced ineffable joy. His friends and relatives are good natured by and large as long as they do not lend money or borrow money from others. They often helped him with their good advice. He got seats for many people in hostels. He got many students admitted into many schools and colleges. He also took up the task of career counselling and instructed them how to pursue certain courses by moulding their golden future. Many students prospered. That was his great satisfaction. The respect earned from students is greater than any satisfaction a teacher gets. His friends grew into his admirers gradually. They treated him with awe. They looked on him as their revered *guru*. He thought that it was sufficient for him in this life.

New desires were springing in his mind. His scooter became old. It was useful for the children. He wanted to buy a car. He did not stop buying it.

He learnt driving a car. He enabled Janaki to learn driving a car. He went to the houses of relatives taking Janaki and children by car. He went to meet his friends by car. He earned reputation in all social circles.

Each age has its own pleasures. He wanted pleasure for each status. He wore a coat and a tie putting on shoes. He changed his style of speaking. He went at everyone's invitation. He presented them with gifts. He poured his money generously on certain occasions. He joined many organizations at their invitation. He read Buddha's teachings. He studied Vyasa's *Bhagavad-Gita*. He read the writings of Dr. Ambedkar. He read the biographies of both Mahatma Gandhi and Jawaharlal Nehru. He acquainted himself with Japan, Germany, America, and Soviet Union. He came to understand two world wars. He knew Indian National Movement. He understood Socrates, Plato, and Aristotle. He studied *Sankhya Shastram, Upanishads* and *Meemansa*. He digested the essence of *Vedas, Ramayana,* and *Mahabharata*. He studied the writings of Nagarjuna, Kautilya and Hegel. He assimilated non-duality theory. He nurtured unusual thirst for study. He studied books with intense interest. He drew essence from the books he studied with avid interest.

He threw away what was without essence.

Long ago a person died leaving a cheque beside him after earning money worth thousands of crores.

He was cremated on a pile of sandalwood sticks. The cheque that he wrote was treated as invalid after his death. Everything would be valid as long as one lived. Alas! that man attracted repugnant rebuke. He earned fame to earn money. He cheated many people. He misled banks. Anyhow his funeral was held in a grand manner. He departed; his wealth remained. His sin departed with him. His wealth remained with his heirs who earned more wealth.

They changed their names. They moved from the villages where they lived. They changed industries. They changed their trades. They changed their shapes. They led their life as the persons who were heard but not seen. They had some differences.

They entered into the political industry from other industries. They stayed in politics. They won the elections. Banks bowed to them. All governments obeyed them. The wealth worth thousands of crores were being accumulated in various forms in their houses. They said that it was a heartache. It was surely the jealousy of people. Though he departed, his wealth remained.

Sathyam was surprised. Why are these mendicant's thoughts for?

"Never think in a big way and damage your brain, my dear." Janaki advised him. Janaki was a remarkable realist. A small family can be without any worries. The children grow satisfactorily in such a family.

What more did one yearn for?

When there were a maid servant and someone for ironing clothes. All were going on as per his wishes. There were no large longings. She was satisfied with twenty *thulas* of golden bangles and other ornaments. She went on buying one by one. She didn't know how to preserve them.

She took a bank locker and kept the ornaments in it. She would take them out occasionally to wear them for attending various functions. Janaki had no more desires than this.

Sathyam had no large longings.

He had no desires. His car was causing trouble to him. It became old with long years of use. He exchanged it for a new car in a showroom. He employed a part-time driver. He charged as per hours he worked and took out the amount from Sathyam saying that it was the minimum. He purchased his old house. He thought of possessing a villa in a gated community. He met the officials at a bank, borrowed money from others and took a villa at last. It was located in a peaceful atmosphere with decent people. He felt very happy there. He experienced a lovely atmosphere in a favorable climatic condition.

Sathyam was very eager to control his desires. He thought that he would never abandon life's essentials as longings. He considered the following basic needs of life. Eating three meals a day is not a longing but a necessity. Having a good house is not a large longing. Having a good job is not a big desire. Possessing good health is never a large longing. These are always treated as the essentials of life.

Sathyam has no great desires. A good slate and a good slate pencil were his basic needs when he was at school. He had no big longings.

He wanted to have a good car and a good villa. He wished that his children would be employed suitably. Besides these desires he had no large desires. He wanted to have the minimum of desires to lead his life.

He treated benevolence as an essential need of life. Why Sathyam is getting new desires in his mind causes a lot of surprise to Sathyam himself.

A NEW LIFE

Sometimes we think that all is over. We can have an opportunity at such a moment. When you smell things properly at the right time, you are sure to get a second opportunity.

We should utilize such an opportunity. When our self-confidence shatters, we can't gain anything. What we hold as a fruit of our action in our hand can slip away from the hand. The opposition is bent on defeating us by all circumstance's protests against us unexpectedly. The people who are ours will be in conflict with us. In such a state your soul and your conscience are in embittered animosity with each other.

Some people stop in the middle. The people who avail themselves of the second opportunity will become victors in life. Though they meet defeat at the initial stages of life, their final triumph can be tremendous.

Another opportunity knocked at the door of Vasundhara. She was not capable of judging things properly.

There was a lurking fear that customs on one side and the scandal mongers among people on the other side would pester her. Life raises hopes for future. Lost life can be regained. Our elders and trustworthy people ensure guarantee. The people say that they can show the evidence about the occurrences of incredible things.

She lost her husband three years ago. When she was a young girl, her marriage was celebrated. She had her daughters married at a young age. With the death of her husband the known and the unknown observed her. When she slipped her leg, he would keep her as a concubine, giving her some money every month. Let her pour some earth on him. Let such a man die.

"Should I feel ashamed when someone asked me to be his concubine? I am the mother of two children. How can I show my raised face to others? How can my children live in honour in such a situation?

This relationship is relatively distant. I don't know the nature of such people there. He says that he has his own house with his children settled somewhere away from him.

He says, "None will interfere in your affairs. Whenever I come to you, treat me like my mother." Can't I know such things? I am a mother of two children. I have performed marriages and celebrated ceremonies. I have seen several things. What will be my fate if my son drives me out of the house? I can't say in these times.

What will be my predicament if someone views me with bad intentions after I go there leaving my children? If I stay here, I will get the strength of my own village. None can expect things there. I can live with any other person except a drunkard.

He says that he has no bad habits.

Does he speak of such things if he has any of them? I don't know how many debts he has. I don't know how the parents of his first wife will chide me."

Vasundhara thought of knowing the opinions of his children. They may say, "Have you no shame at this age?

What a peevish mind you have!"

"You have grown up children. Do you pour dust into our lives at this age? " She remained calm with the fear of attracting such curses.

"Vasundhara, this is certainly a good alliance. You won't get it again if you miss it. A man gets many alliances. Many days have passed. You haven't said a single word. That elderly man has sent me with his message to you again.

Vasundhara was thinking deeply after Laxmirajam told her about the alliance. Though he did not belong to her caste, she called him uncle. Laxmirajam treated her as his daughter. He was of great support to her as he lived in the village.

"It is not misfortune in any manner. It is not difficult altogether.

There are many love cases. After two years of togetherness resulting from elopement arising from love, people are leaving their partners for petty reasons. This alliance is not like that."

Vasundhara thought in such a manner.

"We have a large house. The elders of the village lend their support to me. I can put on vermillion mark on my forehead again. I can wear golden ornaments again. I will roam as a lady without staying in the house. His sons are said to be doing big jobs somewhere. They live at their places of work." She poured such feelings.

Anjaneyulu saw three photos of Vasundhara and approved of her appearance. His grown-up children.

were living on their own at the places of work. His wife, Sugunavathi was a good home maker. She took care of her sons and daughters-in-law, daughters and sons-in- law and her grandchildren very much. She wished to die as a chaste lady. She died of heart attack all of a sudden. Sugunavathi died as she desired. Everyone condoled her death when she was crossing her difficulties. She didn't trouble others. The people who knew her said that she was fortunate. Many women said that she departed as a pious lady.

Her obsequies were performed under the supervision of her sons and sons-in-law. Anjaneyulu saw them as a spectator. Her ashes were merged into the waters of the Godavari and the Ganges rivers.

After the end of the obsequies, the relatives went to their respective places. They invited Anjaneyulu to visit their places for a change of atmosphere for some time.

When he came home, the house sobbed piteously. Everywhere there were memories of Sugunavathi. The value of a person is known to us only after his or her death. He didn't know,

how much service she rendered to him. She looked after him without calling her. She made him dependent on others. She didn't allow him to do anything for himself. She told him that she would do anything for him.

Rajyalaxmi, a maid servant, did household chores including the cooking of food. That was her great fortune. He was avaricious to desire from Rajyalaxmi the tastes that he cherished from Sugunavathi. He burned his hand while cooking food.

He went outside and indulged in gossip. He felt some scarcity at each step.

"When men die before women lead their lives in any way. If the wife dies before, the husband finds it difficult to live." There are some people who pour their sympathy on the men who have lost their wives recently.

The family runs smoothly with the cooperation of women. It disappears in the absence of women.

There are negotiations. The people praise the importance of women in life.

Why do such people weep when female infants are born to them?

A house without a woman is like a house rolling in ashes.

Anjaneyulu's mind was not at peace. He went for morning and evening walks. Though he indulged in gossip till night, he didn't get enough sleep. His well-wishers advised him to go on pilgrimage. Wherever he went he was like a solitary bird. He felt that his hand was broken. Not one hand but two hands were broken. It seemed that life almost neared death. His Sons and daughters-in-laws, their children, and the education of their children- all led improper lives.

He would not go to them when they felt that his presence was displeasing.

Someone advised him to try for second marriage as a widower. Such a proposal caused displeasure to him. It was like doing injustice to his first wife, Sugunavathi. It was like losing his honour in a group of ten people. As the days passed, his mind began bending towards such a proposal. His friends talked about alliances. They said that I would endow a poor widow with a new life. If the woman was a widow without children, he would marry such a woman to get a new life for him.

It would also prove to be a good life for her. If the alliance was from a divorcee, it would be welcome in many respects.

When someone mooted the idea the name of Rajyalaxmi was proposed. Rajyalaxmi was staying in the house as a divorced person. Someone suggested that she would be good for Anjaneyulu in many respects. Moreover, Rajyalaxmi did everything to him. A friend suggested that he should contact her regarding the matter.

"I don't like such a proposal. She is like my daughter. Moreover, she is a fatherless daughter. She treats me as her own father. She is younger than my youngest daughter. "Anjaneyulu said these words.

In the course of his intense search, he came to know of the alliance of Vasundhara. They wanted to know his opinion regarding her remarriage after a lot of thinking. They had to send her the proposal and wait for her decision.

When the matter was around Laxmi Rajam several times, their thoughts turned to Vasundhara. There was no hurry whatsoever.

She would take a decision on her own after judging various things. Things were progressing in privacy.

When all things were favorable, there was a discussion on paraphernalia. Something should be there in her name. There should be security for her in the event of the clamour by her sons. She should refer to Sugunavathi as her elder sister and her sons as her own sons.

She would bring fame for the house and genealogy and keep the prestige of the family as the mother. They taught her several things.

As per the decision of the elders of the marriage Anjaneyulu deposited some money in the bank in her name. The marriage was held in a temple with the knowledge of some people. The new couple thought of greeting the photo of Sugunavathi with folded hands. They obtained marriage registration certificate.

Such was the turning point in the life of Anjaneyulu and Vasundhara. She cooked food for herself. Cooking became her irksome assignment.

The maid servant, Rajyalaxmi, seemed to be his own daughter. He had a support in an unknown village.

She cooked food for three people instead of two people. Vasundhara asked her to eat the food in the house.

Anjaneyulu's affairs were known to his sons. They decided not to go to him. They discussed about the property and went to the village for two days.

Vasundhara felt that there was an attack of a tsunami. Anjaneyulu wanted to call the elderly people of the village. They came to the house earlier than he expected. Laxmi Rajam brought three persons to speak in favour of Vasundhara. There was intense exchange of words. The elderly people spoke of some marriage agreements.

"I got you all educated properly. I brought you up and performed your marriages. I earned the property and the house with my painstaking efforts. If you don't love me, treat me dead on par with your late mother.

Don't come to this house. If you come here, I won't object your arrival. I will take care of you without any deficiency. This property will be your own only after our death" Anjaneyulu said these words decisively.

"I am directionless, Sons. I am like your mother. I have come here to serve your father. I won't take away your property" Vasundhara shed her tears.

The elderly people brought about reconciliation between the two groups. After all the people were pacified, Anjaneyulu spoke to them convincingly.

"If you think of her as your mother after the death of your mother, come here with the feeling that your mother is still here. You feel no dearth. Never forget that this is your house." Anjaneyulu said these words in a conciliatory manner.

"You should have said these words earlier." His sons, daughters-in-law, daughter and son-in-law shouted at him.

"These things are not to be revealed earlier. Nothing has been lost by now." Laxmi Rajam reconciled them all. All elderly people opened their conciliatory voices.

All relatives and children reiterated their past relationship continuing their travels to the village of Anjaneyulu. Vasundhara was a sociable lady. The children loved her as their new grandmother. All people mingled with one another. Rajyalaxmi was there as their own child. Some called Vasundhara Mom and others called her Aunty. She treated all such calls as Mom and acted accordingly. She let others forget their own mothers. For the children she was a good grandmother.

Vasundhara conducted Dhoti Wearing Ceremony for their grandsons and Ear-Piercing Ceremony and half saree Ceremony for their granddaughters.

She conducted them for her satisfaction. Anjaneyulu had rejuvenating enthusiasm. His appearance was radiant with good food.

As the time was passing, she got unusual joy with nutritious food and affection added glow to her appearance. Some called her Old Auntie and Anjaneyulu Old Uncle.

They walked in the house like the new children bringing grandeur to the house.

On the advice of Rajyalaxmi Vasundhara got flours of various kinds on the auspicious occasion of Bathukamma. Rajyalaxmi piled flowers for Bathukamma for her and requested her to come with her. Vasundhara was in a state of confusion. Her neighbouring ladies invited her to take part in Bathukamma Festival along with them. She wore a new sari and went with them. She looked at her face in the mirror rather shyly. She was filled with ecstasy.

As Vasundhara's face beamed, Rajyalaxmi's face glowed. Vasundhara gave the saris of Sugunavathi kept in an almirah to Rajyalaxmi for wearing.

Rajyalaxmi wore such saris and decorated her with flowers. She thought of her as a young lady suitable for begetting the children.

Vasundhara asked Rajyalaxmi to get married again.

"I won't get married. I will stay with you. If I get married again and go with someone who will render service to you. Old Auntie, I will stay with you." said Rajyalaxmi.

"I have got married again. You should take my example. We can lead our lives on our own." said Vasundhara.

Anjaneyulu said those same words.

"All resemble him. I look for a good man. If you wish, I will find a man who can come here and live with you." said Anjaneyulu.

"No, Old Uncle, I will stay with you. I will live here serving you at my best" said Rajyalaxmi.

"We will be always with you, Rajyalaxmi, "said Anjaneyulu.

"Later I will serve my brothers and their children and live here till my death." said Rajyalaxmi.

Those words were capable of bringing tears into the eyes of both.

Vasundhara and Anjaneyulu. Rajyalaxmi was a brave girl. She was scared to hear the word of remarriage from them.

The new old couple was not prepared to hear the sacrifice of Rajyalaxmi. She was an innocent lady. She was afraid at the expression of marriage as she was reminded of her past life. When they were happily married for the second time Rajyalaxmi wished to be alone.

Her decision did not allow them to be asleep during the night. They thought that times would change unexpectedly. They deposited some amount in the bank in her favour. They looked for some alliances for Rajyalaxmi.

They told an elderly man that they needed a divorced man for a lady who has no one to look after her. A divorced man responded to their proposal by saying that he would purchase a taxi car with their support and pay the debt on his own. They had a fixed deposit in the name of Rajyalaxmi. They were desirous of getting a loan sanctioned on the fixed deposit account of Rajyalaxmi and for the remaining amount of the loan they were prepared to stand for surety. The bank assured them of the sanction of the loan.

At first Rajyalaxmi negated the proposal. I won't go anywhere leaving you. She accepted their proposal and told them that she would not leave them under any circumstances. She requested them to stay with them. Anjaneyulu and Vasundhara asked them to live in the two rooms. At their consent Suresh was very elated. Their marriage was celebrated in a small temple. Within ten days they were the owners of the car.

After some time, Anjaneyulu's sons and other relatives felt that it was good that Anjaneyulu got married. His marriage facilitated him in many ways. Otherwise, he would have to stay at a place for three months and move to other place for living there for another three months. His daughters and daughters-in-law were joyous.

Though Vasundhara worked for others gleefully and was tired enormously, she was filled with new enthusiasm. Vasundhara's children came to the house to meet her on some occasions. They called Anjaneyulu Dad. Anjaneyulu was ecstatic to hear such a call from them. For formality's sake he presented them with new clothes and deserved the name of Dad. Some months passed. Rajyalaxmi and Suresh gave birth to Lasya who became the darling granddaughter of the old couple.

Vasundhara served Anjaneyulu with the forbearance of Mother Earth at her. During the summer vacation all were in the house for ten days. It looked like a festival.

Sometimes Vasundhara's children and grandchildren were in the house on vacation. Vasundhara was a bit afraid that the people would think otherwise. Rajyalaxmi mixed with all kinds of people and united them. Within two or three days the elders
and the children were together.

Vasundhara was not the same woman. Her patience decreased gradually. Anjaneyulu found fault with her on some occasions.

Rajyalaxmi said, "Old Uncle, entrust any work to me. I will do it for you with pleasure."

Anjaneyulu and Vasundhara exchanged words on one occasion.

She said that she could not tolerate his words. She said, "How can I serve a man, who is unsatisfactory? I have grown old."

" You are a directionless woman. I will see how you lead your life. "He shouted.

Vasundhara was unable to bear the humiliation at the hands of Anjaneyulu. Her grief knew no bounds. One day Rajyalaxmi tried to stop her from going away. She really went from the place weeping bitterly.

Rajyalaxmi felt scared. She made a call to Anjaneyulu's near and dear.

None came to see him. They told him that they had no holidays; he should take care of himself and take assistance from Rajyalaxmi.

Anjaneyulu remembered Vasundhara and sobbed piteously.

"Come to me, Vasundhara. Where have you gone? Elder Son, where have you gone? "These loud cries of Anjaneyulu caused fear to him.

Vasundhara went to her daughters because Anjaneyulu scolded her. She was not able to sleep properly at night.

Rajyalaxmi sent her husband, Suresh, to find Vasundhara at her daughter's house. Suresh went there and brought Vasundhara back by his taxi car.

At the sight of Vasundhara in the house he lifted his folded hands.

"I never speak a word against you.

You shouldn't go anywhere from here onwards." Anjaneyulu said with tearful eyes.

"How can I go anywhere leaving you?" Vasundhara said shedding tears.

"What has happened now, Old Uncle? She came to know that her daughter was unwell. That's why she

went there to see my sister." Rajyalaxmi brought about reconciliation between the two groups.

The neighbouring women came there to speak to her when they came to know of her arrival. They praised Rajyalaxmi by saying that it would be fortunate for people to have a daughter like Rajyalaxmi.

" Whatever you speak you remain united. You will be here till the growth of our children. Finally, two people will become old. Whoever may depart is unpredictable." The neighbouring women said these words. "Lasya is growing old. Lasya should give birth to a baby girl. We can't say how long we will say." Vasundhara smiled at their words.

Sometimes we think that all is over. We can have an opportunity at such a moment. When you smell things properly at the right time, you are sure to get the second opportunity.

MY VILLAGE

When I took my mobile handset trying to make a call to Sujatha,

I saw a WhatsApp message sent to me by Godavari.

"Sorry, Sujatha," I said with fury bursted on Godavari.

"Sorry, Sujatha, it has been a long time as you have said. We travelled by an old jeep there. We haven't gone there since then. In those days all villages seemed alike. On that day there was no proper road and there were jolts which almost broke our waists. You suffered from the strain of thigh.

Is there no tar road to the village?

Can we go there by an Innova car comfortably. If we perform the journey to the village in the old manner it will take three days to go there and return to our homes with a day of halt at the place. Now we will go there and get back to our homes by tonight. You say that there will be no people to ask us to stay there for a day as we did earlier in those days. You say that we should go there to meet all people, take care of that work and come back home.

You say that we can go there and come home comfortably in an Innova car.

The son of Chinthakindi Lachanna,

Sanjeev, must have grown more than you by a cubic. Nowadays the boys are growing high enormously. We had no luxuries during our childhood. Now they eat luxuriously. Sanjeev took post-graduation degree from Osmania University. He wrote Railways, Bank and Group Examinations. He will get some job.

Sanjeev was persuaded by Lachanna to marry a girl of her choice. Has Sanjeev no interest in such an alliance? Whom can we convince? Father or son. Is Sanjeev staying on the campus without leaving the house for that reason?

I do agree with you. That it is true.

Does your sister agree to such a proposal? Does Lachanna go ahead with the agreement?

Sanjeev likes Prathima. Prathima likes Sanjeev too. They formed their association in Osmania University.

They worked together for Telangana Movement for several times. They visited Landscape Garden together.

Their tours and discussions united their minds.

They are really majors. When they like each other, we should approve of their alliance as elderly people. If we can't do so, they will plan elopement and get their marriage registered disregarding our eldership. You say that it is good for us to celebrate their marriage with our presence. That will be nice.

Does your elder uncle stay calm?

Does the village remain under the *jagirdar* system? His son has emerged as a great builder. Why do they still act as dictators? Recently he has stood as a candidate for Z.P. T.C elections and was defeated.

Hasn't he learnt a good lesson? You say that he is envious of the triumph of Chinthakindi Lachanna in the open.

How can such a man remain silent when we wish to perform the intercaste marriage of Lachanna's son with his daughter? Think over the matter seriously. We may attract adverse criticism by undertaking such a good thing.

well. Theiree Harika and the boy committed suicide because their parents rejected their marriage proposal. Whenever we remember such a tragic incident, our minds get agitated. The grown-up adolescents, properly educated, should have planned elopement and subsequent marriage. She loved her parents very much. She had great attachment with her parents. They committed suicide thinking that their elders didn't understand their minds well. Their parents have lost them and are weeping now. We should not be like such parents. Let us convince their parents and celebrate the marriage of Sanjeev and Prathima. Your lofty ideal that we should persuade the people of the mandal to agree to the proposal of their marriage reveals your good intention.

We should give moral support to them. We will have to wail if we lose them. I can understand the agony of your heart.

Let us go ahead in this matter. I am glad that Jahnavi, Sita and Ramesh

will come with us. If we do not get the work completed, we will return shame faced. Then we will forget our sweet memories. It won't be so. The village has changed a lot. The people have changed considerably.

You have said that large lights have been arranged at Rachabanda Chowrasta with the funds of A.P. Lads. A library was set up at the village. Three hundred rupees are to be paid towards a dish connection.

So what? The whole world has come into the village. How can we call a village? Everyday milk vans are being driven to Jagtial. Two thousand and seventy students attend their classes in the schools of Jagtial. You say that there is a rural bank in the village.

Though Hyderabad is at a distance of forty kilometres we call our village a city. Our village is not at a distance of ten or twelve kilometres. How can you call it like the old village? The statues of Mother Telangana, Chakali Ilamma, Sardar Sarvai Papanna,Konda Laxman Bapuji and

K. Jayashankar have been installed in the village. You say that consciousness has grown. Now you say that the marriage of Sanjeev with the Velama girl,Prathima,causes happiness to the village as it is not a new thing.

Let things go on as you wish. I will advise my husband to cook food for himself for two days. We should go there in an Innova car chatting gleefully over several things.

If negotiations are fruitful, we should hold the engagement on the same day. Does Z.P. Chairperson, Uma, come on time? You have a mastermind. Let us go. This is a righteous action.

Tell Sanjeev about our decision.

Prathima should be informed. He should be along with his friends at Jagtial. We can facilitate their marriage registration with their engagement photos. They should keep ready their dates of birth certificates. Ask him to tell the matter to Prathima.

Sujatha had unprecedented enthusiasm after going through the message sent by Godavari on WhatsApp.

After fixing the programme she arranged a conference call to Chinthakindi Lachanna, Sanjeev and all.

RELA

"What is caste, Daddy?"

Chary looked into the eyes of Rela who asked the question.

Thirty years ago K.N. Chary and Allam Narayana lived at Giripuram near Mogalrajapuram, Vijayawada.

K.N. Chary and Sulochana and Allam Narayana and Padma resided at the place.

Giripuram colony was famous for the book-binding industry. There was an old house at the turn of the street.

There was a tree and cool shade in front of the old house. The talk of caste emerged while he was sitting in a cot on the platform, discussing with his daughter. Discussions were being focused on the political power to be obtained by B.Cs., S.Cs and STs if they were united.

Chary responded to the question of Rela in a remarkable manner. How can we grow tomorrow's children in a responsible manner.

"How should we grow the children of tomorrow above caste and religion? This question was there in the past. It has been raging a controversy till today. The question should be proved with practice. Until the mindset is changed, no new cultural values will be stabilized. We can practice a new culture through habits and associations. When new cultural values are stable, human relationships go beyond the spheres of caste and religion. Human relations, values, culture and blood relationship grow naturally. The society is as fascinating as the society. When such a society is formed there are no disparities between the rich and the poor. When will we see such a society? We should be hopeful to see such things in our lifetime." Chary said as a way of reply.

" How good you have spoken! "

Prabhakar complimented Chary.

"As we live as one family Rela has grown beyond the considerations of caste and religion. "Chary's eyes have shone with the pride that he is growing his daughter without the knowledge of caste.

Daughter Rela went to school.

Sulochana brought him tea stopping her sewing machine. Rela was the beloved daughter of Chary and Sulochana. She was a lovable girl to many of his friends. All liked her, her childhood, and her intelligent questions. She was the girl, growing in their hands and laps. There were teams without knowing the smell of caste and the smell of religion.

"I feel overjoyed to hear the questions of Rela. It would be nice if our children grow without the discrimination of caste. It will be a new society." Prabhakar praised Rela.

That day's discussion on castes moved on the screen of the eyes.

Whether the society is progressing or receding is not known to us. In those days intercaste marriages and interreligious marriages were ideals.

Such couples who liked each other and married are now celebrating marriages identifying themselves with a caste. Alliances are arranged on caste basis.

"Rela has become a bride."

This was the caption under the photo of Rela posted by Ajitha of Eluru fascinated Prabhakar. It brought about the memories of past thirty years.

The photo of Rela as a bride posted on Facebook by Ajitha showed the light of her childhood and self-confidence in her eyes. Her eyes were radiant with the self-confidence with which she would win the partner of her life.

Prabhakar looked at the photo again. " Are those his own feelings?

Are such feelings expressive in her eyes? " He said to himself.

Chary passed away a long ago. How Sulochana was leading her life was not known to others but to herself. How she was facing hardships to grow her fatherless children was known to Prabhakar. Her childhood was like that. Her father died when she was a child.

Her mother took care of her education and marriage. Sulochana found her vocation in tailoring. She worked in a sacks company for some time.

Sulochana stayed at Buddhanagar, Warasiguda, Secunderabad.When. When. When Chary died, I went there and saw them. I don't know where Sulochana and her children lived.

Friendships remain sound with frequent meetings. A journey for half an hour is sufficient for such purpose. Meetings in a city are difficult. I wish to meet several thousands of people in the city.

We wish to meet at least one hundred people. How many friends can be met at their homes? In this large city one is said to have four friends. He has one hundred friends.

A lot of work consumes our time.

Many problems arise in life.

Chary had great dreams about life.

When he was studying on O.U. campus. When he was unemployed,

Devulapalli Amar, K. Srinivas and he published a magazine, *Vooru-Vaada,*

to motivate *sarpanchs* for building a rural society. He brought out many magazines and volumes. A magazine cannot survive for a long time when marketing is not promoted.

The inauguration of *Jeevagadda* was interesting. B. Vijayakumar and Ramulu wished to bring it out. Things did not progress as per their wishes.

The registration process for the name of the magazine was executed in New Delhi. The secondhand printing press in Hyderabad was kept in operation with the payment of advance. Things happened in that manner. Lives changed a lot, turning imaginations upside down.

Chary and Allam Narayana agreed to be sub-editors for *Jeevagadda,* A daily newspaper to be published in Karimnagar. There was a team comprising Chary, Allam Narayana and Vijay. The cooperation of Sharada Printing Press was unforgettable. If there had no cooperation from him, the paper would not see the light of the day.

Jeevagadda started as an evening paper and created history.

Vijayakumar departed and Sabita and Reena remained. Sahu associated with them in the office of *Jeevagadda.*

It is a new world at Karimnagar. That office is itself a new world. It represents a family. Naradasu Laxman Rao, Varala Anand, Gopu Linga Reddy, J. Manohar Rao, Pendyala Santhosh Kumar, Chitrika Puranam Ramachandra, Navatha Chukka Reddy, Narendar Rao, Annavaram Devendar, Ghanta Chakrapani, Naredla Srinivas etc were in affinity with the editors, K.N. Chary and Allam Narayana in running the paper.

Chary and Allam Narayana learnt lessons in journalism and taught the first lessons in journalism and Telugu words to be used appropriately in

various situations. The paper, "Jeevagadda", gave life to the journalists more than 350. Then Amar worked as a staff reporter for Andhra Prabha. He became the first president and the General Secretary of Journalists' Association. The cadre of journalists spread far and wide in the state. The journalists, the poets and the authors born with the support of *Jeevagadda* joined various newspapers.

Chary-Sulochana and Allam Narayana-Padma came to Vijayawada from Karimnagar. They had great joy for getting jobs in big newspapers and had pain in learning a new language, which was not their own. The associations of Vijayawada made them forget that pain. Affection wove around them like a creeper without causing an obstacle to their speech. Lime kilne center, Navodaya Colony, Mogalrajapuram, Bank Colony, Giripuram, Chandram Building, Puttumacha Khadar, Nekkalapudi Usha Rani, Andhra Prabha Subramanyeswar Rao, Indian Express M.Chandra Shekhar,Usha, S. Danny, Eluru Ajitha, Yuvaka, Nancharaiah, Apsar, Nagendra Press Babu Rao,His daughter, Mani, Venu, Karuna, Chukku, Vemana Vasantha, Jagan, Anuradha, Pattabhi, Gopal Rao, Daily K.Ramachandramurthy, Vijayawada Vijaya talkies Nakkal Road, Eluru Road…The creeper of friendships went on spreading in such a manner.

That was the period which witnessed experiments in newspapers. Udayam, Andhra Jyothi, Andhra Prabha, New columns in Eenadu, New news, New analyses, the days expanding, the experiments growing on one side.

There were discussions on all matters. Book reviews, new views in conflict with old views, Analysis paper management, Babri mosque, Rama Janmabhoomi, Common Civil Code, Conflict of views about Karamchedu, Unending discussions on the solution of problems, Perestroika, Glasnost.

The world capsized all of a sudden. The conflict of views, The entry of new views, Gradual unification of BC, SC, ST and Minorities. They went by pages, sessions and days. With the perspective in mind Rela has put the question.

"What is the caste, Dad? " Suddenly that question occupied the mind.

Rela must have got the answer to her question after she got married.

"Does the question require any response? It is the best thing that the question remains unanswered.

What is poetry? How can we answer our children when such a question is put to us? Some does not attract definitions. Some does not yield to definitions."

" How can we define the mother? How can we define the father?

We can find definitions in terms of words but no reactions. Words never awoke reactions. Meaningless words do not create reactions in us.

Will it not be good if the word, "caste", remains unanswered? It should not evoke any emotions in such a situation. Then society will grow enormously. When will it be possible?

How will it be possible? " Prabhakar poured his thoughts in such a manner.

All of a sudden there is Facebook news.

Rela had no deprivation though she was a fatherless girl. Her friends stood by her on the occasion of her marriage. Eluru Ajitha, M. A. Khan and the Yajdani couple acted as maternal aunts and uncles. Allam Narayana, Chairman, Telangana Press Academy and Allam Padma Couple bore marriage expenses. Prabhakar was surprised to read the news. In the month of May,1984 Allam Narayana and Padma had a meeting marriage.

There were people who did not find a difference between a meeting marriage and a traditional marriage as the meeting marriage was performed ostentatiously. Prabhakar thought of performing the marriage of his sister in a grand manner. Muddasani Kanakaiah and Ajitha exchanged garlands for marriage.

In 1994 Advocate Koravi Gopal had something unusual about his marriage. He tied *mangalasutra* in a stage marriage. Bojja Tharakam and Shivasagar wondered at the way the *mangalasutra* was tied in a stage marriage. The weapons of yesterday would become the ornaments usually. Cannons were decorated before the office of Tahsildar. *Mangalasutra* and toe rings were treated as the symbols of a slave in ancient times. They are now considered ornaments. They have become definitions of marriage. The married girl and the unmarried girl are viewed differently in our society.

The view of the bride was respected till she was matured. The villagers were astonished at the way meeting marriages were celebrated instead of sacred rice flowers were sprinkled over the couple to bless them suitably. There were many types of marriage. There were many occasions. The society went on changing on various occasions. Despite the social constraints Padma-Narayana and Ajitha-Danny were united in wedlock as per their opinions as the childless parents adopted a child. This was certainly a novel experience.

It is new culture to unite various religions to perform marriages traditionally. It certainly showed the amalgamation of old and new. Relationships were established beyond castes and religions. Intercaste marriage is a historical necessity. The young men are getting such marriages performed to suit their interests. To perform such a marriage in a grand manner is their dream.

Why should we celebrate joyous occasions in the manner the people are observing nowadays? We should yearn to be happy like other people. In B. S. Ramulu's story, *Bandee,* the hero desired to have an intercaste marriage. Some people add reality to their dreams and such heroes are growing in number. The young people are getting their marriages performed by their parents preferring intercaste marriages to

traditional marriages. The heroines were not afraid as Renu in the story,

*Bandee. T*hey should be as brave as Rela who has succeeded in convincing her parents. Birth takes place in society. The lotus rises from the mud. A new society emerges out of the old society. What we desire can never be fulfilled. What is going on is not as per our wishes. We should accept truths and invite new orders.

This occurred in the case of Rela. It is an unforgettable experience for those whose marriages are performed in a traditional manner though they marry beyond caste and religion. Why people distanced from them when they marry against the customs of caste and religion?

Prabhakar complimented Rela in his mind. Rela won the love of all unifying all castes and religions on one occasion. Prabhakar has thought of conveying his best wishes to the new couple on the auspicious occasion of their marriage.

There are some more photos on Facebook. All the people expected are present on the occasion of Rela's marriage. Except Prabhakar all have attended the marriage ceremony.

He should go to their house to bless the couple. He has searched for the mobile number of Eluru Ajitha to make a call to her with a view to finding their house. He has not found her mobile number. He has made a call to Danny and found the mobile number of Eluru Ajitha. He has got the mobile number of Sulochana from her. He has wished to get the mobile number of Rela from Sulochana. Prabhakar has thought whether she can recognize him.

Prabhakar has made a call to Sulochana. They seem to at the marriage registration office for marriage registration. They have discussed various matters. They have invited each of them to visit their houses. The marriage registration certificate is ready. Sulochana has said, "I will call you again, Brother."

Prabhakar has said, "My best compliments to Rela and the new couple." He has kept his mobile away.

THE VICTOR

"We feel desperate when our excessive hopes and objectives become futile. We develop inferiority complex from disgust and despair.

This condition aggravates our anger and despair. With these unwanted developments we forget victories.

We look down upon them. We should respect what is accessible to us. We should remember such victories and enjoy them. We should reduce our failures, hopes and objectives to a large extent. We alone cannot achieve the things that can be achievable through the cooperation of ten people. If someone revolts against us by winning our trust and cheats us, it will be an irreparable blow in life. With such a blow life undergoes modification. When we go wrong at a stage we need not worry about life. We are subjected to deception in life on account of our greed. Our avarice is the chief cause of sorrow in life." Siddhartha said these words.

"Is it avaricious to become a doctor, take dealership and undertake contracts? " Suryam revolted.

"You need not be angry, Suryam. Do you wish to become a doctor, take dealership and take up contracts for your sake or for doing service to the people? Is it for earning money or for social? status? Tell me the answer directly."

Suryam felt irritated. That question seemed to stab him. It seems to be great to others. We can earn some money. This yearning is the root cause of desires. When he faced such a direct question, he treated it as an insult.

"Have you understood me in this manner for such a long time?"

Suryam flew into rage all of a sudden.

Siddhartha saw Suryam till his anger disappeared gradually. It looked as if there was pitter patter on tin sheeted shed. The jasmine creeper swung from here and there emitting sweet smell.

" There is nothing wrong in the thinking of Hemalatha. It is a natural desire of women. Her father has a wholesale shop. They have many cloth god owns. There are shopkeepers with the clerks moving from here and there. Hemalatha was born into such a wealthy family. That you are cheated is the reason for your anger. You leave the man who has cheated you and show your anger towards her. You use words unnecessarily."

Suryam's face was reddened. The legs, the hands and the body were trembling with fury. He was breathing heavily as if he was suffering from heart attack.

Some people left hot tea and snacks on teapoy. With the cool breeze blowing with the smell of jasmine flowers the hot tea and popcorn caused glee to the mind. Siddhartha tasted the sweetness of tea and tried to say that the tea was good.

"Yes, the tea is good but these jasmines are very special to Hemalatha."

"In an unexpected rain they have sent a good thing by sending snacks and tea."

"Yes."

"It is joyous when things are available to us though they are hoped for."

"How is it irritating when we do not get things which we hope for half an hour? Then we will forget the sweetness of tea."

"It is true."

"We do not digest things entirely when we don't get things at the right time. There may be anger, dissatisfaction and impatience, we should not lose patience. In Jo Biden's life there were many unhappy incidents and failures. Take for example Abraham Lincoln. Also take the example of Ambedkar. Their lives passed through many trials and tribulations. There were many upheavals. Many opportunities slipped away. They were not disheartened. Finally, they were crowned with triumph. We should have the strength of determination.

Why should we be disheartened?

If you can't run, we should be satisfied with what we have to lead our lives happily.

"Do you say so?"

"As the eldest son of the house you accessed things on time and didn't get many within the stipulated time.

On account of deception, you faced you did not get satisfaction in life.

To be the eldest son in the house is either a boon or a curse. You can treat things in such a manner.

To me I won't get pleasure and satisfaction in this life. Why do we waste our precious time indulging in such a discussion? Let this life go on. I don't know how many desires I gave up. At last Hema says things in such a manner."

"Suryam, since you have yearned for a lot of things you can't get sufficient satisfaction and joy in life.

Your brothers and sisters have a lot of respect for you. You have nothing less in life. Your son is an engineer in America. Your daughter is a doctor.

You got them educated in various states. You have sold away all your land. You have a well-built house which fetches you a rent of twenty thousand rupees. You have a scooter and a car. You are healthy. What more should you long for? You saved the life of your father as the eldest son of the house. You protected him from a murderous attempt made against his life out of factionism. I know the truth that your life has made several turns. You thought that your father was your support. None can forget your noble deeds. After the departure of your father, you celebrated the marriage of your sister fulfilling your responsibilities as a father. You partitioned the property as per the wishes of your mother. You have made many sacrifices as the eldest son of the house. Though your brothers didn't recognize you your sisters are aware of your sacrifices.

The world is conscious of your nobility. The property grown by the father melted away. Great landlords spent their properties for education and marriage. They were reduced to the middle class. This will not pose a problem to you. You have lived up to the reputation of your family. You wish to grow more. Circumstances should be conducive to you. Can the sons of the Prime Minister grow to the stature of their father? That is impossible. That is not inefficiency on the part of such people. Objectives, aims, circumstances and generations go on changing. Compare yourself with your classmates. All of them are leading happy lives like me. An own house, lovely children, good health and respect in the society are all that we require in life. In the age of innocence we grew dreams about our golden future. We had rich imaginations then. Changes and reciliations are common when we grow in age and experience."

"Whenever things happen contrary to our expectations we should be reconciled to our lot. Mother often told me that I was the eldest son, and my brothers and sisters were very young and advised me to be tolerant in all matters. She often backed them on all occasions. Whatever work I did for them remained unending. When I said to them," I have made many sacrifices for you." They said with disapproval," What have you done? You have sold away what our father earned." They would raise their voices against me. Then I would tell them that I had left several things in saving our joint family. When I got good jobs, my mother wept saying that I would go to a far-off place leaving all my young brothers and sisters." How can we celebrate the marriage of your sister, Swathi?

How will your brothers live when you don't show them paths? Your father had already departed. If you leave all of us, they will get spoiled." She wept bitterly. That was why I left all my hopes and found a job near my native place. Siddhu, you don't know the problems the eldest son faces in a family. Have I led my life as I have dreamed? It was difficult for me to lead a life for the sake of my brothers and sisters." Suryam had inexplicable agony which could not be understood by others. Then his mind was filled with fury.

" Suryam, now you have no mother.

Your father died a long ago. You have stopped talking to your cheats. After the death of the father, all disintegrated families are united. Circumstances, personalities, and generations have changed. They still think that they should have grown further. Hemalatha saw all things in his life. She also made several sacrifices. When you feel that you have made so many sacrifices, Hemalatha might feel that she has made sacrifices on par with you as your wife. Why can't you realize her virtues and sacrifices? When the children have grown a lot, the credit should be attributed to you."

"Siddhu, you don't know what she has done. You say that she has done a lot to others. She often asks me what I have done to her. What should I do to her when I have shouldered such responsibilities? Did I purchase kilos of gold to mend all these things? How could I do good things to Hemalatha in a joint family? First of all I would have to work for the welfare of my sisters. I undertook a job belatedly. The salary I got was insufficient to meet the expenditure in the house. I sold away my property for the sake of the education of my children. How should I purchase things for her when she asked me for them like a dragon fly?

"Suryam, these things should be understood by everyone. First of all, take care of her desires. Respect her and praise her good nature. Let her understand that you have sacrificed for all people. She will understand your greatness. Hema is not a small girl. You are worried that she can't understand your sacrifices. She is also worried about how she has suffered a lot in life with you. Doesn't she know that the man who brought about an alliance between you and her cheated your money amounting to twenty-five thousand rupees for gas dealership? Twenty-five thousands of that day is more than twenty-five lakhs today. When we cajole them for telling them things, they will go away from us. What will be useful to us in such a situation?

What is the use of leading an unsatisfactory life by conflicting with the desires of childhood? This kind of life doesn't return to us. Suryam, keep her matter aside.

You are not low in any manner. Keep all such things aside. Compare yourself with your classmates. All are leading happy lives in your status with an own house, good children, good health and respect in a group of ten people. At a young age you read books and saw the films. Then you imagined that you should be like such an actor. Whose mistake, was it?

It thundered somewhere. The tin roof vibrated unexpectedly. The smell of jasmine was thrown.

There was tumult in the heart of Suryam.

"Suryam, the imaginations of childhood woo us immensely. If good things take place, it is okay. We must look for joy and satisfaction in this life. What is the use of a hunter's anger regarding the escape of the stag which he is hunting? It can't jump into his lap suddenly. Ours is a lovely life. We have accessed the things within our reach. What is inaccessible to us can be out of our reach. We should think that it is not our own." Siddhartha said.

He adjusted in certain situations. He took such things easy.

He is irreconcilable. He forgot many things. Suryam thought that Hemalatha's eternal conflict with was incomprehensible. He adjusted in various matters. In the distribution of the property, he adjusted himself to certain situations.

He spent a lot of money which remained unaccountable. It was not his nature to get a question from his brothers about the expenses. Hema didn't understand certain things.

"You should forget your male domination and think from the side of Hema." Siddhartha went on saying things to Suryam to convince him to the extent possible.

"What you are saying is true, Siddhu.

What you are achieving seems to be natural. Never forget that you have achieved these things with your hard work. You are dissatisfied over the unachievable things looking down on the things you have achieved. What is within your reach is not of little value. Your sacrifices are in no way trivial. The life you are leading is not less." Suryam said.

" We can find satisfaction in life without nurturing the thought of recognition." Siddhartha said.

Suryam argued that he had no such desire.

"Abandon such things. Why do you worry about the past? What we have achieved in life is not insignificant. We have won the lives for our children. We have fulfilled the duties of our generation. Nothing remains unfulfilled. We stood firm in the face of overwhelming odds. We are certainly the victors of lives." Siddhartha said.

" Do you say this? "

"How can you lead good lives? What we have achieved is not less.

Let us give up our failures and additional desires. We got our children educated at various places.

with small salaries. Though our promotions were scarce we were victorious over our lives." Suryam agreed to the proposal of Siddhu finally.

Siddhartha heaved a sigh of relief.

The rain stopped. There was no sound on the tin-roofed shed.

Someone brought tea for them. With tea there was the fragrance of Jasmines in the air.

"Hemalatha has sent them tea twice without asking her for tea. She is also good." Siddhartha praised her.

"Hemalatha is hospitable to a large extent." Suryam laughed.

"We don't need other things. She has sent us tea for the second time without asking her. With her presence she creates a heaven in the house. Suryam, you are the most fortunate person in the world."

Siddhartha went on singing a song in a low voice.

Suryam was reminded of several sweet experiences of his childhood with those words. He laughed heartily for some time. He smelt the fragrance of jasmines.

"Yes, we are victorious over our lives." Suryam shouted hilariously.

When Hemalatha came into the open from the curtain Suryam felt shocked. He was afraid that she might have overheard their conversation.

"Have you heard all the things, Hema? " Siddhartha greeted her.

After many days the eyes of both Hema and Suryam met each other.

A SHATTERED DREAM

A dream has shattered.

"The news should be a lie."
But he told it to me over the phone.
My cousin met his death.
My young aunt's son
Hanged himself to death.
Why did he hang himself to death?
The fact is not known to us.
He looked good in many ways.
He often mingled with all people.

    My young maternal aunt's dream was shattered. She had four children.
    The growth of the family stopped all of a sudden. She lived her life fully.
    She was reconciled to her lot. She got herself adjusted to her life. Though she suffered from various things she was not afraid of them.

My broken-hearted uncle died a long ago. My aunt gathered courage

and led her life in her house on her own. When she was in a helpless state she lived with her sons for their support. They were all good natured.

They had scanty selfishness. They longed for a good house in a town.

amidst dear and near. It seemed to be a wealthy family. Three brothers occupied three portions and led happy lives.

My aunt passed away three years ago. When my aunt lived my cousin found great support in her. She had a lot of self-confidence. When his mother died, he lost his self-courage.

He treated himself as alone man and rode his bicycle with a bundle of clothes.

He used to go to four villages and sat near his sewing machine. He stitched clothes. He stitched a suit and gave it to me with a lot of affection. He was a man of innocence. He was fair and frank. His ears didn't function effectively. He is known for workmanship. He got married. His wife was good natured. They had two children. She used to make beedies.

She sent her children to school. I thought that my cousin was leading a happy life with his wife and children in his house though their life was not characterized by growth. All of a sudden there was news which was like a thunder bolt from the sky. One of the cousins made a call to me saying that that cousin of mine lost his life.

He didn't die normally. He hanged himself to death. No one knew why he hanged himself to death. How did such misfortune haunt him? He left his wife and his children in a state of gloom. It was not known what he thought of himself, his children, his wife and the world before committing suicide.

His death was a fact. The reasons were imaginations. His house was good to look at. His family was very small. Whenever he went there, he was greeted affectionately. What happened to his heart. It was not easy to comprehend his heart. His suffering was beyond explanation. His life was beyond growth.

There was no hope of growth in life.

He had some education. His children did not receive higher education. Such education didn't provide him with food. He left for gulf countries for livelihood.

It was the region of the gulf. It was the region of mirage. He didn't know what he was doing there in that desert. It was not known whether he paid off his loans or not. None of children got married. When they got suitable jobs, He would think of performing their marriages. Suddenly

my cousin departed from the world.

Why didn't my cousin obtain the tolerance of my departed aunt?

My aunt and uncle were the ideal couple of my dream. They were my parents when I was fatherless. They led an ideal life. They provided their assurance to me to lead my life securely. They gave me all the support and strength for leading my life.

My uncle went to Bombay to work in a textile mill. He was tired of working in the textile mill. He went to his house. He thought of practicing medicine and got deceived. He collected his courage and went to

Kadem project. He started a Kirana and cloth shop. He spent three decades there till his children grew up. He opened cloth shops for his children. Old age refrained him from leaving his house. He started his journey to home. He didn't stay calm.

He went on manufacturing the spare parts of the bicycle. It was a burdensome task in decrepit age. I was glad to know that my uncle and cousins had established an industry.

In this competitive world, commission and attraction are better than quality. Expenditure for collecting money is greater than profit.

That was why the industry stopped its functioning. The doors of new employment to my cousins were closed.

My cousin who completed graduation scrambled for employment. My eldest cousin thought that he should join the cloth shop instead of searching for a job. Days passed by. Years passed by. The children grew up.

The cloth shop was incapable of providing employment to all. Annapurna Cloth Store kept its name as it didn't expand itself. As a result, they came from the village to the town.

My uncle purchased some land. He built a tin roofed shed. He started cycle spare parts industry. He thought of building a house. I advised him to grow his shop for investment.

" Should you have a house of his own after such a long time? What should I say? Investment gives employment. A house gives us shelter. They gave prominence to shade. A beautiful house came up.

Everyone has his portion. They got shelter but not employment. Their investment was exhausted. They lived within their means. Their children grew up.

They had no support from others.

In seventy years of independence uncle, aunt and the brothers lived independently. They lived with self-employment. My aunt made beedies as long as her hands and legs worked well. She opened a small grocery shop at home. She led her life forward with self-confidence.

She witnessed many travails and witnessed grown up lives which halted for a short time. One family gave place to four families. Hers is a lonely life. There were five families altogether. Growth was not unusual.

There was nothing unusual about employment. Moreover, the house was electrified. All children were educated well. None got good employment.

They went to the nearest cities in search of employment. There was no stable life. There was no employment security. There was a feeling that that day and that year should pass, and that festival would be celebrated. There were many worships. They used to eat their meals with ten people. Those were the joys left over.

There were birth ceremonies and first hair-cutting ceremonies.

Life went on like that. An average Indian life and an average Hindu life.

Those cousins were average Indians.

My uncle started development process at the age of seventy. It stopped with the arrival of my cousins on the scene. They studied well. They had their own business activities. Their wives wound beedi leaves for livelihood. None would sit idle. Their children grew up. When they attained marriageable age their marriages were performed. Later they also had children of their own. Three generations passed by.

I thought that he would restart his stopped life. He lost the cloth shop.

He lost a bundle of clothes on his bicycle. Tailoring was the only means of livelihood for him. He had a house and children. He died suddenly. He hanged himself to death.

What happened to this world? Why did he hang himself to death without reasons? The reasons known were a little. He killed himself.

Thus he ended his life.

Whose roles were there in the suicide of the cousin in seven-decade long social transformation? Why was there no growth in his life? Why didn't he and his children get good employment?

He didn't come up in studies. Did all educated people get suitable jobs?

Forty years ago, my cousin who passed the degree examination was incapable of getting him a job. He went to the Gulf. He came home exhausted. His younger brother followed the path to the Gulf.

What happened to this country and this society? I was surrounded by many families and many relatives. I found

Japtapuram on one side and Venkatapuram on the other side. I also found Korutla on one side and another village on the other side. Progeny grew within seventy-five years. Generations grew up. None was capable of growing up. Why?

My father took the path to Bombay.

My uncles followed his path. Later they went to Bhiwandi. Some settled at Siricilla. One generation passed.

Next generation arrived. Similar life.

Nothing was achieved with education. Nothing was lost without education. Life stopped without any growth.

In almost thirty families one or two could show their growth. Were the lives on the bottom line similar in India? They were led for a morsel of food from hand to mouth. What happened to self-respect, self-confidence, development and skill development?

Has our nation advanced?

Where are my people and my cousin? He is not motionless. He is at work though he is dead on account of hanging. What happened to him? Where did he stop? How did his dream shatter? What dreams did he bear? What dreams did he have? This country has its dream for future shattered.

My cousin hanged himself to death.

The generation which has no hopes for future is hanging itself. The young generation in this country is hanging itself. Does anyone hold responsibility over it? Everyone has his own way of life.

He is responsible for his death.

None is held responsible for it. My life is my own. This life is enough. My cousin felt that he could not live further. That was why he hanged himself to death. This country is hanging itself. My dream has shattered. The dream of this country remains shattered.

THE FISH

Our batchmates and hostel mates often make calls to me. It seems that you are busy. The life you are leading is not your own. One can derive genuine joy from his profession. Profession should constitute a part in your life, but life should not become a profession. What kind of life are you leading? There are streaks of years behind your laughter. Do you think that I am not capable of judging between the tears of joy and the tears of sorrow? The fish in the sea lives in the sea alone. When you say that it dies when it comes out of the sea, I can't say anything. The thread of the kite of my life has slipped away from my hands. Take it into your hands. Those days should come back. We should realize our games.

When I see you, I obtain great joy on one side. I am envious of your games and leaps on other side. You consider it actions. Is it an action?

The source of the marriage of both Nagarjuna and Amala was action.

Is togetherness the source of marriage? Meenakumari and Kamal Amrohi, Nargis and Sunil Dutt, Dharmendra and Hemamalini and Vijaya Nirmala and Krishna were united in marriage on account of their togetherness. As there is living in togetherness there are experiences.

Without experiences there is no togetherness.

Those days were different. In this wide world we should cook our own world with all facilities. There were quarrels over the curries cooked.

You wept bitterly on such occasions.

I was merciful towards you. I felt some dearth when I was incapable of speech or touch on such occasions.

We hugged each other firmly. We didn't know how many times we did such things. We kissed each other.

The spectators knew how many times we kissed each other. We saw certain scenes repeatedly on You Tube. When I saw such scenes on You Tube you were not there. I was not there beside you. Suddenly you sent the video as a message to me on WhatsApp.

Sometimes mental pleasure is superior to physical pleasure. It is surprising that you have written similar words. Before we entered the courtyard, we were different people.

We planned to win the game without thinking of our bodies. When there were competitions, we were separated while teams were formed. We looked unhappily under such circumstances. Many people smiled at us.

I ran with great speed on your intimate insistence carrying you in my hands.

I thought that you would fall down slipping from my hands. I hugged your head firmly. We intended to win the game without thinking of our bodies then.

When we were tired, we indulged in gossip. At such moments there was a meeting of the eyes and the legs. You were there tidying your hair.

You were pressing your head saying that you had a headache. When I fell down receiving injuries in the game

you kept yourself awake with me. Then I was moaning with pain.

After training you attended interviews. You fascinated many cine and television directors with your charm. During training there was a competition for you. Your loveliness

fascinated them. You grew as a glamor star all of a sudden. How did such individuality disappear?

Where did you hide such beauty?

There was sexual harassment. Were you free from casting couch? You know that Vineeta left the field on account of the sufferings of casting couch. Our Sougandhika has settled in the television films. Vaishali

is running her own tv Channel besides playing some roles in soap operas. Anand has got settlement in

a reputable firm as the C.E.O. The witch of words, Malini, has become Anchor Malli. Ravindranath has joined CNN. That depreseed lion has gone into the cave. When will it come out of depression? Visharad is still acting as Regional Manager. Adithya is distancing himself from others. That firebrand is now a brazier without fire. Anandi has remained single. Lata Mangeshkar has said that she has an ideal. She wishes to dedicate her life to the profession without any hindrances.

You should have remained like her.

What kind of life is this?

When we stepped into the courtyard, you and I were strangers.

In that environment our games and sports and angers and competitions separated us keeping us in two different teams. There were looks of separation. We smiled at each other.

There was joy in the game. We hugged each other several. times.

Of us who took more intimacy? It is not known. The electric bulb shines with the union of two wires. The emotions and moments were eventful.

Were the moments in which our hearts met and melted a part of the game? Didn't we know that many crores of people were viewing the programme live?

Those moments were unforgettable.

I am leading this life with such experiences. When you hugged me by saying to me "Come, Shiva." I thought that such experience was enough. There were many people in our batch. We were the only two to have such a bond of union.

During our training we played and sang only for the sake of game. Didn't our hearts flower with such games and songs during the training ? Our

individualities became butterflies and flew away. We learnt how to share love in a group of ten people?

Your half knickers, topless tops, casuals, pants, shirts etc enriched your elegance. If you keep quiet, your beauty speaks. I am a bit uneasy.

Let us quarrel between ourselves.

We spread our beauty in the swimming pool.

There were many wanton quarrels.

There was sulking. Suddenly there was love. If we don't talk, the mind was not quiet. That was why there were willful quarrels and screamings... I wished to live with such memories.

Tell me truly whether the games we played and the songs we sung were just for the sake of play. Aren't they a part of our life? How can they be training for personal development If they are not a part of our lives? Where can the past go? It follows us.

How many promises have we made?

They are not explained by means of words but can be. conveyed through the eyes.

You married him of your accord. You are saying now that those were your weak moments. What is the use of saying such words now? You didn't contact me for advice. You were led by external glitter and were tantalized without knowing his depths.

I won't hinder your development like him. I remember you that you should become my lovable deity. I knew that your husband had a concubine and many vicious habits.

Who knows that your life is like this?

I am adjusting myself with you all.

I don't wish to separate you. Your married life should be ideal to others.

What kind of life is this? Those who have no opportunities will be destroyed. Think over whether you are utilizing opportunities for your advantage. What has come over your

personality? Glamour is not permanent. Personality is certainly eternal elegance.

I haven't become popular like you.

We have a lot of things to share for our living in togetherness.

If you leave him, we should start a new life in togetherness. Those days should come back. I will be happy if you live a separated life like Anandi. Then your life will be better than the present life you are leading.

How many people are living in such a manner? There are several people around you. I intend to see glow in your eyes again. Your personality should gleam again.

Yours sincerely,
Unnecessary Shiva

GURUKULAM

"When I come back, wash my clothes. Boil the dhal. I will season it after I return." Sujatha said these words and tried to depart.

"Today I will go for work. You should wash linen and cook food for us."

Saying these words Prathima got ready to go.

"Why do you wish to go for work?

Do you want me to be scolded for sending young children like you for work? " Sujatha said these words.

"No, I have some work with Mother."

"What work have you with Mother?"

" Let me go and tell you the things.

later."

"What will you tell me if I ask you.

why hasn't Mother come? "

"I will tell you that Mother is down.

with fever."

"If you say things in that manner,

both of us will not be allowed to enter the house thinking that it is Corona fever."

"I say that it is stomachache."

"Okay, take this bowl, given to you by Mother yesterday."

" Okay" Prathima said before her departure.

Prathima was studying at a residential school. When she was selected for admission into Jyotirao Phule Residential School she felt ecstatic as if she got employment.

After she joined the school there was a change in the manner of her speaking. Language changed. As it was English medium through which she learned and spoke English. Her neighbours praised Prathima very much. On account of nutritious food, she received every day, her appearance glowed enormously. She was growing like a corn stalk rapidly.

In the wake of Covid-19 the government-imposed lockdown in the country. There were prohibitory orders regarding the outside movement of people from their houses. The curfew was clamped during the nights.

All schools and offices remained closed. It was not known when they would be opened.

After some time, offices were opened. Half of the employees were allowed to go to their offices for one day and the remaining half attended the next day. Prathima waited for the schools to be reopened. They were not reopened. The months of March and April passed by. Summer and the rainy season departed. Time was passing. Prathima was waiting for the schools to be reopened. There were online classes for students. Lessons were taught with the use of mobile phones. Prathima was disgusted to listen to those lessons.

Prathima intended to contact Shashank for he filled in her application form for Entrance and got her admitted into the school. Shashank's daughter, Hansika, made her learn many matters in her preparation for Entrance examination. Prathima wanted to grow like Hansika, studied seriously and obtained a seat. She wanted to ask Shashank a question regarding the

reopening of schools.

Prathima was disgusted a lot and asked him a question. When Hansita called Shashank Dad, she called him.

"Uncle" though she used to call him.

" Sir ".

She said, "Uncle, when will our residential school reopen? I feel bored at home. We also miss our online lessons. "When she called Shashank " Uncle", her tongue faltered a little. She wished to say "Sir" but avoided saying the word.

Shashank observed her call curiously.

"How dangerous is it to stay with students during Corona times? " Shashank explained things.

"Sir, may I ask you one question? "

She gave up calling "Uncle" and called him "Sir". Shashank observed it.

"You may go ahead with your question." Shashank said to Prathima.

"Sir, government employees and government teachers are receiving salaries without work. You have received your salary for three months without work. Thank you, Sir. The government is spending one lakh for my education per annum. It gives us free education from KG to PG. We should be paid mess charges every month. We hear online classes. It is difficult for us to lead our lives at home."

With those words Shashank was deep in thinking. He thought that the children would think logically.

"The government should do it in such a manner." Shashank praised Prathima.

Prathima thought about her teachers, classmates, and the school.

She thought that she missed many games and sports and lessons. Her birthday would fall on the day after tomorrow. It would have been grand at school. Had the school started, I would have two rounds of lessons. Hansita was studying her class. At a private school there was a burden of fees and a burden of books. Games and songs were less. Hansita used to ask herself. She learnt how to conduct classes at school. Prathima thought that Hansita would work hard to learn how to teach students.

" Good morning " Prathima said stepping into her house.

"Good morning " Shashank said smiling.

"Good morning Hansita." Prathima greeted stretching her hands to Hansita, who was practising handwriting. She stood up to shake her hands with Prathima.

" Good morning, Mother " Prathima greeted her mother.

"Prathima, you have come now. There are more dishes and clothes." Swaroopa said.

"Mother has stomachache. She has asked me to go." Prathima said these words and dried dishes into the balcony.

"Alas, why haven't you worn a mask?

Do you cause Covid-19 to all of us?"

Swaroopa kept a mask for Prathima on the table. First of all Prathima put the clothes into the washing machine. She went on sweeping the floor with a broom.

"Never go to the room of God."

"Mother, I have taken bath and come here."

"Look at her. What has happened,

Hansita? You haven't taken your

bath yet. Prathima has already taken her bath. Take your bath now."

"We are in the habit of taking bath in the morning. By this time, They provide breakfast to us." Prathima said.

"If she is admitted into any residential school, Prathima will learn all things." Swaroopa praised Prathima with smiles.

Prathima wiped the floor after cleaning it with Lizol. She washed dishes and dried two trips of washed clothes.

Prathima eulogized Hansita for obtaining a rank better than that of her. Hansita got eighty-five marks whereas Prathima got seventy-five marks.

"Hansita will secure good employment. How courteous and cultured she is! You should study well. Our teacher will be helpful to you." Swaroopa said.

"Okay, Mother." Prathima wiped her hands and stood there.

Swaroopa gave Prathima four idlis and sambar in a plate.

Prathima said," Mother, how should I eat with a mask? "

Swaroopa laughed at her.

"You have become intelligent after going to the residential school."

"Mom, we find the sisters elder to us. We learn things from them."

"Take off your mask and look at a distance."

"You have given her before me. Where is mine? "

"What work have you done? she has cleaned a cart load of dishes. She Kept the clothes in a washing machine and dried two trips of washed clothes. She mopped the floor. You have not cared for them as you are educated."

Prathima lost her tiredness after she won praises from her mother. Taking her tiffin, she tried to sit down at a distance.

Swaroopa said, "Your clothes will get spoiled. Sit on that stool."

Swaroopa knew that it was not good on her part to keep young children sitting on the floor. Prathima ate her tiffin and washed her plate. She wore the mask again. She stood there with the intention of asking her mother something.

"Mom, day after tomorrow is my birthday. At our school birthdays are celebrated in a grand manner."

"We can celebrate it at home."

Mother said.

"No money. No new dress."

"During the Corona times no one has got money. Let us ask our teacher who has a lot of money nowadays?"

On account of the lockdown imposed
during Corona times she worked for two months and received a full month's salary. Prathima stood near Shashank who was reading the newspaper. He looked at Prathima when he heard her footsteps.

"Excuse me Sir, Day after tomorrow is my birthday. I need two thousand rupees only. I will pay the amount in four installments."

The manner in which Prathima asked him the question surprised him. Prathima grew rapidly. How much confidence there was in that question! Such humility and such culture enabled him to praise her.

" Give her the money, Dad " Hansitha
kept her arms around the neck of her father.

Shashanka kept four five hundred notes in her hand. "In the amount one thousand rupees is my gift on the occasion of your birthday. Moreover, you are conducting classes for
Hansitha."

Prathima said," Thank You, Sir."
with a sense of gratitude. She tried to run away from the place thinking that the work for which she came was completed.

"Come early in the evening. You should teach me a lesson." Hansitha said to Prathima, who nodded her proposal and walked towards her house happily.

She saw vegetables on the way and purchased them. She bought postcards for writing letters to her friends. Her mother was stitching some clothes on the sewing machine. Prathima thought that cooking was over.

She took out her telephone and dialed to Principal Suhasini.

After receiving two calls Suhasini lifted her phone.

"Good morning, Madam."

"Good morning, Prathima. How are you? Are you studying well? "

"I am studying well. When will residential schools reopen, Madam?

It is boring at home." Prathima said.

"We can't say definitely when the risk of Corona decreases. Why are you speaking Telugu? I have advised you to speak English." Suhasini questioned her.

"If you speak English, you will get enough practice in communication skills."

"Okay, Madam. I will speak English with Hansitha and her father hereafter."

"Are you teaching Hansitha? "

"Yes, Madam. They gifted me on the occasion of my birthday. I will celebrate my birthday at home."

"Wish you a happy birthday, Prathima."

"Thank You, Madam. I am writing birthday greetings to my friends on their birthdays."

"Okay, Okay, Congratulations "

Prathima made calls to her class teacher and P.D. madam and spoke to them. After speaking for half an hour, she felt that she was at Residential School.

Sujatha was stitching her old cloth.

She said," Eat if you are hungry."

"Mom has fed me with idlis. My stomach is full of them. I will cook vegetable curry today. After cooking the food, I will eat lunch."

Prathima often taught her mother English words. Sujatha also learnt English words from her.

"My Mom" Prathima said showing two thousand rupees given to her by her teacher.

"That's why you wish to go home."

Sujatha said to Prathima gleefully.

"Our teacher has given me a gift of one thousand rupees. I will buy a new readymade dress. I will take Hansitha to select my dress. Many fashions have come." Prathima said.

"When will your schools reopen?"

"They will reopen only after Corona decreases." Prathima said.

Sujatha thought about her daughter's going to school in the event of the decrease of Corona.

as per the wishes of his daughter. No one would trust that Kalyani was responsible for that misfortune.

" How is Sameera ? " Acharya Brahmaiah said.

Ramesh thought that all was well with her, and he attracted all the blame.

There was the sound of thunder. He was startled thinking of that thunderbolt fell on his heart. Power supply was cut off then. Chinta Ramesh opened the window.

"There is intense rain. Tin roofed shed has attracted pitter patter. Phone remains inaudible."

Saying these words Ramesh kept the phone on the receiver.

"We have grown hearing stories and songs and viewing films. During our childhood we heard stories narrated by our grandmas and grandpas. *Panchatantra,* stories,

Balamitra, Chandamama etc were very interesting in those days."

" Disneyland and children's films were based on such stories."

Ramesh rested in the chair. Many characters influenced him. He cast such roles in his life for some time.

When he read tragedies, he thought that he was on the brim of death. He felt that he was reborn at such moments. His father departed. His mother also passed away. He was alone. When he came across the incidents of his life in certain writings

he thought that they represented his life in reality. He thought that he stood as an ideal son and father. His daughter thought of him as a bad father. She thought that her father would not agree to her marriage. He imagined how such a small girl like her required early marriage. Should she elope with her fiance after hearing such words. There were many people and many words uttered and heard.

There was steady rainfall. Ramesh dialed his phone. He had a elephonic talk with Dinesh. Similar words. Similar gossip.

"Have they got satisfaction in real life.

though they have done enough?"

SHADES

Chintha Ramesh lifted his head from the book which he was reading.

It was raining outside. The tin roof of the verandah attracted pitter patter. He opened the door and took into the house the clothes dried outside. He took the book again. Books were his friends in loneliness.

When he read the book again the characters in the book would become his friends. It seemed that they would walk into his life as his friends. All of a sudden a new idea would strike his mind. He made a call to Ramesh to discuss the new issue with him.

There were no replies to his two calls. He made a call to another number. He was in line with Brahmaiah. He was very eager to speak to Acharya Brahmaiah.

Kalyani went to her son. Her daughter, Sameera, eloped with her fiance. She asked her parents to perform her marriage with the man whom she loved. Kalyani opposed her proposal vehement They got their marriage registered. They insisted on the recep function which was denied by Kalyani and friends. Sameera birth to a daughter. The baby child resembled.

her grandmother. Kalyani went to Sameera's house to s He attracted defamatory remarks on account of non-perform the marriage of his daughter. He would have performed her

"We can't be treated as good people though we have done a lot of things.

All films and novels have their respective ends. We know the extent of roles in them. Life is not like that.

Some people may think of us as villains and vicious people. My son may think of me as a villain. He may consider his mother an angel. She wins her loyal love. She made my son hate me. What should we do now?

Some people are like that. The inmates of the house and the relatives have no satisfaction."

" That causes me a lot of concern.

Leave the concerns of others aside.

Look into the affairs of the house. Have we done anything less?

How less have I done to Kalyani?

My salary and my life have been sacrificed to them. I am not addicted to drinking and smoking. I haven't gone to hotels. I have no expenses of my own. I have become a spoilt man to myself. I kept them in the city for studies. I myself cooked my own food."

Chinta Ramesh poured forth his worries. Dinesh was similarly situated. Some people speak things openly. Some can't say things. We think that the people who keep their feelings to themselves are very happy.

THE STRINGS OF HEART

The soft and mild sunshine of the evening illuminated the surroundings.

In its gentle glow, some memories came flooding back.

The inner layers of the mind were shaken.

She had been careful over the years not to give anyone the initiative to ask such a question.

But these precautions did not work in Anusha's case. She also needs a person to open her heart to. She didn't know why, but Anusha seemed to be her daughter, who is very dear to her. Anusha reflects herself.

Three-bedroom apartment on the second floor. A cool breeze blows from the balcony. The trees are swaying.

"Madam, why didn't you get married again?" Anusha's question still resonates.

The innocence and affection of Anusha's words brought tears. She pressed her eyes to prevent tears from appearing. It is true. If there were people who would ask like this, she might have really gotten married again! Then some convictions arose - goals of life, the obstinacy of "can't we live without marriage?" Is marriage necessary for life? She thought about how marriage, which hindered the development of a person, was considered so necessary. Can't we live alone in society? Why is marriage considered the highest point of life only for women? Isn't marriage that necessary for men?

Professor Manjulatha expressed her concerns, **"She is getting married is the biggest mistake of her life.**

Is it necessary for the research student, Anusha, to tell what happened? I think it is not good to sow the seeds of aversion to marriage in Anusha's mind unnecessarily. I have nothing to hide from Anusha. I don't know how Anusha will take them." She then slumped back on the sofa, closed her eyes, and remained there.

Silence pervaded the hall.

The sound of the fan spinning filled the air.

She slowly opened her eyes.

Her mind still overwhelmed with thoughts.

Choosing an unknown person as a husband in the matchmaking interview...

The process of selecting a lifelong partner seemed flawed.

After marriage, there seemed to be no other option but to adjust.

Why was it necessary for women alone to compromise? They had entered the relationship with love and hope for a happy marriage, but divorce didn't even cross their minds. As they moved forward in life with determination during their youth, that strength now appeared to be waning.

Loneliness and solitude weighed heavily, something they couldn't reveal to anyone.

A person needs a companion because the mind requires support. It's terrible when the mind dislikes the companion they have.

In her life, she made a mistake once and is determined not to repeat it.

When a man and a woman live together, they discover what's truly on their minds.

Everyone seems to be good at first glance, so it's easy to make friends.

Love may appear genuine, but its authenticity may only be revealed when intimacy is involved.

Domination begins.

She desires companionship with a like-minded man rather than remarriage.

She waited for such companionship in friendship, but when someone came forward with an initiative, she seemed suspicious and kept her distance.

Body is important for them. Physical happiness is important.

She values the connection of hearts and minds with her companion.

However, these things may not matter as much to men.

Prof. Manjulatha thought about how to explain these things to Anusha, who was not married and not old enough to fully understand.

After recovering from her tragic mood, Prof. Manjulatha tried to smile.

Anusha thought it was not appropriate to ask her about things she might not like.

"Sorry madam…did I hurt you?

Prof. Manjulatha reassured Anusha 'Come on... You are the daughter of my heart. You are my reflection dear... The question you asked is also a question I often ponder myself'. Professor Manjulatha groaned in her mind.

Nothing, madam," said Anusha. "There was a marriage alliance the other day. My Parents insisted that it is a good alliance. They have shown the biodata and the photo. They told me that he is a lecturer in government college. Everything seemed fine. I still want to study, and I don't want to get married until this Ph.D. is completed."

"So, are you wondering how it will be after marriage…? Why, madam got divorced, why she is single...!" Manjulatha laughed, coming out of her thoughts.

Anusha also smiled, with an expression of affirmation.

She made green tea and served her.

"Green tea is very nice," appreciated Madam Manjulatha.

Anusha observed how madam's mood was. She recalled how beautiful madam was at the age when she fell in love! Why didn't madam put the photos of those days in the hall? She might have thought to erase all the old memories. Madam is maintaining her physique beautifully enough to believe that she is not yet married.

There was a half-blossomed smile on her lips when she remembered her friends asking her if madam was her older sister when she went shopping with her.

"Madam! The alliances are not for me. I have brought you an alliance, madam," Anusha said, laughing heartily.

"Alliance for me!" Madam also burst into laughter. She placed her hands on Anusha and shook her in astonishment.

The atmosphere was lightened.

"Madam! I was told that a D.E.O. met my father unexpectedly. It has been a long time since his wife suffered from paralysis, and she asked him to look for a cultured woman who would help both of them and marry him again. My father said to ask you, madam," Anusha said, looking at her with agreement.

"You mean after such a long time; I have to go as a step-wife for someone! Even if you know the reason for the divorce, you and your father would bring such an alliance?" Manjulatha laughed.

"Who can be found unmarried persons at this age, madam?" Anusha asked curiously.

"There can be divorcees! There can be widowers!" Manjulatha smiled naturally in response.

"Madam! Haven't you come across such persons all these years?" Anusha asked directly.

"Why didn't I meet them? Shouldn't like? The mind keeps pulling back, thinking that the difficulties of the past will be faced again."

"Madam! Why did you get divorced?" Anusha asked straightforwardly.

Anusha was not innocent at all. 'Active girl,' Professor Manjulatha thought, noticing how she inquired about everything with a smile.

A Hindi song was telecast faintly on some channel. How many years has it been since Lata Mangeshkar sang that song! Even after 50 years, the sweetness of Lata Mangeshkar's voice has not diminished at all, even today.

Anusha went into a trance, mixed with the song and scenes of "E mere watan ke log." She witnessed the soldiers guarding the borders of the country, struggling in the snow and dying in minus 40 degrees temperature at the world's highest Siachen battlefield in the Himalayan Mountain range. She saw scenes from the Kargil War, the march past, and soldiers carrying wounded comrades. She also witnessed the guard of honour by the military officers to the martyrs, including Prime Minister Jawaharlal Nehru's bouquets and salute to them. The series of old and new scenes played before her eyes, including the recent incident of 15 soldiers getting stuck in Siachen in a snow blanket and the tragic scene of Hanumanthappa who was found still breathing under the snow even after five days. She also saw the futile attempts of doctors to save him and Prime Minister Narendra Modi paying tribute to the martyrs.

In breaking news, Anusha saw the agitation of students and hunger strikes in support of Rohith Vemula, who committed suicide in Hyderabad Central University. Demonstrations of students in universities all over the world were also shown.

As the song ended, more visuals appeared.

Anusha came across incidents of gang rape, which disturbed her patriotic heart deeply, leaving her groaning in pain.

Unable to bear the distressing scenes any longer, Anusha changed the channel.

However, she found that everywhere, there were scenes of sexy dance songs..., as well as scary breaking news being reported on various news channels...

Many people are sacrificing for the country, but the citizens show indifference and neglect towards them... political speeches by leaders... the heated discussions on TV channels.

What does the future hold for the families of those who sacrificed their lives for the country?

Can anyone replace the role of a father, husband, or son? The TV channels seem to have no time or concern for these matters, and this raises conflicts and confusion in the minds of the Indian viewers. It's disheartening to see the level of selfishness in some individuals.

Manjulatha came out of the bedroom with a few books and placed them on the teapoy, she said, " Anu! Look at it once" and handed one to her.

They look like diaries. Anusha asked the same thing. Madam! Aren't these your diaries? Why are you giving them to me?

"Read, dear," said Manjulatha, "You don't have to read them all, but the answers to your questions can be found in this diary. Keep turning the pages, and you'll understand at least a little of what happened in our lives."

As the room's lighting was dim, Anusha switched on another light.

She turned down the sound of the TV channel.

Professor Manjunatha slumped back on the sofa, closing her eyes. Some scenes from the past life were moving in her eyes, and she remained silent in such a state.

Anusha hesitantly took out a diary, her hand shaking a bit for reasons unknown. Perhaps the feeling that reading someone else's diary is wrong. The fear of what she would have to read on one hand, and on the other, there was curiosity to look into madam's life.

The sound of rapidly turning pages in the diary mingled with the sound of the fan.

"Read slowly, there is no hurry," Madam Manjulatha said with her eyes closed.

How many years Anusha went back... you would not have been born by that time.

"What an imagination... how much love... how many chit-chats... how many hopes..."

Anusha closed the diary and heaved a long sigh. With the sound of the diary being closed, Madam Manjulatha smiled, looking at Anusha, in agreement with half-open eyes.

"Madam! You loved sir so much... your chit-chats... hopes... how well you wrote! You would have been a poet, madam..." said Anusha and smiled appreciatively.

The bursting sound on the TV channel was like a bomb blast. Manjulatha further reduced the sound.

"Madam, why did you break up after loving so much?" Anusha asked curiously.

"If there were no hopes and expectations, the need for separation would not have come," said Professor Manjulatha. "There are not many expectations and hopes in arranged marriages and the alliances set by the elders. People make a compromise that it is enough if the married life goes on. Only after thinking in this way, the alliance seen by the elders will be confirmed. Therefore, they each compromise a little and drag the chariot of married life. Love marriage is not like that. It is difficult to bear if those who become intimate with many hopes, goals, lots of love, and friendship change after marriage. I couldn't bear it when those hopes, and love were not fulfilled after marriage."

She took out one diary out of four and gave it to Anusha, saying, "Read this diary.

If you read this, you will know why we broke up."

Professor Manjulatha remained just watching Anusha.

While turning the pages of that diary, Anusha felt nausea in her stomach. Some horror scenes were moving across her face as she read the diary.

The diary is full of frustrations, depressions, and crushed self-esteem due to male domination.

How she was mentally tortured, with suspicions about her fidelity and his blustering nature.

How he would grab her entire salary, displaying an intolerance that did not respect her as a human being.

His belittlement of madam, suicidal thoughts...

The moral support given by two lady friends...

The way of gaining self-confidence... approaching the court for divorce...

Tragic sentences like poetic lines...

" Madam, even if all this happened, did none of your people support you? " Anusha asked, unable to contain her pain, wiping away her tears.

Madam smiled sadly and slumped back a little more on the sofa, stretching her legs over the teapoy. Thus, leaning back, she fell into thoughts.

"I did not write in the diary because I did not want to write bad about them. Everyone tells me to adjust myself... There is no one to tell him to change his attitude," she said.

When the past was remembered in fragments, she suddenly got up and went back into the bedroom as if she remembered something. She searched in the almirah and brought a letter.

It was a letter written by Madam's father. She read it and was shocked. "Are fathers like this too, madam?" asked Anusha.

"Whatever it may be, madam. You should have got married again. Get married at least now."

"Even those efforts did not go well."

She took out another letter and gave it to Anusha. It was a letter written by a younger brother to an elder sister. She was shocked after reading that letter. Anusha was somewhat suspicious of the love and affection she had so far towards brothers and fathers, so she asked about it.

"Have you read the story 'Alarasa Puttillu' written by Kalyanasundari Jagannath? In it, she wrote about an elder brother who deceived his own sister and killed her for the honour of their clan and about their attitudes," Manjulatha said, continuing to narrate the story in a nutshell. Anusha felt some fear.

Anusha recovered from fear and mustered strength.

"Has that sir got married again, madam?"

"Do men have any problem? Someone comes forward to marry or give their daughter in marriage. He also has two children."

"Have you ever seen him? Did he show any remorse?"

"Yes, I have seen him. **His repentance is for his benefit only.** I will be happy if you come back to me. Our doors are always open. My wife has no objection since you are employed. Moreover, my wife says as she has no children it is more advantageous for us. You will have all the rights as the first wife. She is like your younger sister. Such dialogues ran for a few days. I cursed him rudely and stopped talking."

There was silence between the two for a while...

Madam Manjulatha reviews her life once again. He wants to have children, but she doesn't. He doesn't want her to attend the meetings, but she wants to. All the opportunities for him. Her situation is inevitable. The end result is it tragedy.

Tragedy along with success in reaching the goal.

She thought she must give up some for the goal.

She gave up her life and reached her goal. She lost her life.

In olden days, the proverbs were not just originated. It was not merely said that what should be enjoyed at certain age should be enjoyed at that age. What is the use of thinking now? She reached the target but lost a life. Lata Mangeshkar also might have remained celibate for the purpose of reaching her goal. Maybe she didn't want to get caught in various bonds.

Anusha asked as the scenes of the sacrifices of the brave soldiers, Lata Mangeshkar's song, the soldiers who got stuck in the snow in Siachen and became martyrs for the people of the country repeatedly move in her mind.

"Madam, it is similar in the case of the Prime Minister Narendra Modi also! He has given up his family life for the cause. Don't misunderstand me, madam. Isn't your goal a part of selfishness? You moved forward to reach your goal with individual thinking. Isn't it selfishness?"

It is true! As Anusha said, it seems now her goal is a part of her selfishness. Then her aim was to achieve something in life. Then it did not seem selfish. After knowing that, she wanted to adopt one. Her younger brother's selfishness, asking her to adopt his son or daughter…

In the countries of Europe, America, and Australia, the institution of marriage and family is decreasing. People are living together as long as they like. They have their own earnings and houses. They stay together like friends and even have children with their loved ones without getting married. As a result, around twenty percent of the youth are growing up in those countries. This method has also started in our country. But this, in turn, puts the burden on women, and new problems are emerging. "No, that is not correct," said Madam Manjulatha as she kept on talking about the lives of one or two of her students living without marriage, the hardships they are facing, and their loneliness.

Different weddings, different experiences… There is no less risk factor in everything. We cannot say it is good, that is bad. Ninety out of a hundred marriages arranged by elders survive on compromise. **If there is a chance to survive after separation, more**

than half of those who had traditional marriages would have divorced. They are living in self-deception in the name of responsibilities and children's future, with a painful heart. They are in a sorrowful situation that they cannot claim that they are living in such a state. Has omniscient experience reduced her to an unappreciable stage? She thinks.

After a while, as if she had come to a decision, Madam Manjulatha looked at Anusha and said, "Give me the boy's biodata and photo."

She remembered what Anusha had said, "Madam, what do you know when you see the biodata and photo? What do you know if you talk on the phone? Moreover, what do we talk about to new people? What will they think if I talk too much...? They think that the girl is shrewd."

Madam Manjulatha replied, "That is why match-making interviews are not correct. Befriend a person for a while. He should be observed. Know their friends and relatives. It is difficult to know everything no matter how much you try. We don't know how they will change after getting married."

"Madam, don't we know some information if we choose from classmates or colleagues?" said Anusha.

"It is true, but they are not as good as they seem. The true nature of people comes out after a long time. Selfishness becomes the ultimate goal of life, as everyone is driven by their own selfish motives. Humans lack the vision to care about the whole nation and country, and mutual cooperation is not seen as a way of life and perspective for most people. Instead, narrow-mindedness and cooperation for personal gain have become prevalent. This has led every individual, class, and caste, even those who appear highly cultured, to be driven by vicious selfishness. They exhibit irresponsibility towards society, engage in corruption, misuse power, participate in the black market, and promote black money. Expecting others to be as highly cultured as they claim to be might not be possible unless they live as wickedly and selfishly as they do. The idealized culture of the elite is based on vicious oppressive exploitation. If someone questions or tries to eradicate this exploitation, the layers of their ideal nature are removed, and their real natures come out." Madam shared all her life experiences, resembling counseling sessions.

"Adopt me as your daughter, madam," Anusha asked, smiling. "I will be your aid."

It is 8 o'clock at night, and Professor Manjulata is observing Anusha. She thought, "What a beautiful physique, how humble, and what modesty!" Manjulatha remembered herself in that demeanour.

Anusha did not want to leave madam alone in her sadness.

"I will cook for both, madam. I will be here today."

"Look if there are any vegetables in the fridge."

Manjulatha changed the TV channel, turning her gaze towards the TV and then towards Anusha.

While Anusha is cooking, the tempering smells delicious. It seems that madam Manjulatha has increased the TV volume.

Some Hindi song sounds melancholic, like "ye duniya, ye mahfil mere kam ki nahin..." Then Lata Mangeshkar's sad song... It appears that while listening to the songs, Manjulatha is reading a book and taking notes.

Anusha, who had been observing Madam's thoughts, searched on the smartphone and showed it to her. Manjulatha took the cell phone into her hand and carefully observed everything: the data he had kept in the marriage bureau, his hobbies, the visuals he was watching on Facebook, the discussions he was having, and his friends of friends. Madam Manjulatha scrolled through everything for a while.

After reading Madam's diaries, Anusha felt some fears. Despite these fears, she finished cooking. Anusha couldn't settle her thoughts about her marriage. Should she like a person first and get married to him later? Or should she get a person married first and later like him? Moreover, she wondered why divorces were taking place despite love and marriage. She questioned why Madam had to get divorced even though she loved and got married.

Anusha arranged plates and dishes on the dining table.

"Come on, Madam, let's have food," called Anusha.

Recovering from the mood of sadness, Madam Manjulatha got up and said, "I will come after taking a bath."

After taking a bath, there was some brightness, radiance, and confidence in her face as if she had decided something. Manjulatha had looked twice at all the details in the biodata given by Anusha.

"The boy is a gentleman," agreed to the marriage.

"Madam, another proposal has come. The boy is working in the Indian Air Force. My father doesn't want that alliance. It is up to your decision which relationship you settle," said Anusha, laughing comfortably as if her burden was over.

Anusha was serving rice and curries, saying, "I don't know why, but I am scared, madam. You call two or three times and talk to him, and then tell me. I will come to a decision after talking to him myself."

"The attitude of men is not changing even though the generations are changing. It is a good relation among the available ones. Call on the phone and talk to him. The biodata is fine. He also looks good in the photo," added Anusha.

"O. K.," said Manjulatha. Today's children are evolving. She looked at Anusha satisfactorily and appreciatively.

"So, I will agree only if you adopt me as your daughter. If you give me the opportunity to accompany you as your own daughter in your home, you settle the marriage proposal," said Anusha, her face blossoming with the never-before-seen glow of the joy of a wedding.

"That means I have to find out the son-in-law of this home!" laughed Professor Manjulatha.

Professor Manjulatha had seen such happiness in Anusha for the first time. She put her hand on Anusha's shoulder and embraced her. Anusha thought that she had never seen such happiness in madam. Little did they know that it was mother-daughter ecstasy.

15 May 2016;　　　　　　　　　　　　　　"Bathukamma"
　　　　　　　　　　　　　　　　　　NamasteTelangana
　　　　　　　　　　　　　　　　　　　SundayEdition
　　　　　　　　　　　Vedagiri Rambabu Birthday Story Issue

OSMANIA UNIVERSITY CAMPUS

The atmosphere of Osmania University Campus will always attract you. Once you get used to that atmosphere, you won't feel the need to go home. However, if you do go home, people will ask you to work as a teacher in a private school. This could feel like dying in obscurity after living so nobly, or you may face criticism from others as an unemployed person. Additionally, there is societal pressure to get married. Consequently, many students hope to stay in the OU Campus until they secure a good job. They choose to stay on the campus, taking up part-time jobs to earn some income, and continue pursuing postgraduate degrees after postgraduate degrees, including research. Many students follow this path, and Arun is one of those individuals.

Some of the students who are currently studying at Osmania University Campus, Hyderabad, were previously students of Ramachandraiah, the Principal of Women's Degree College, Jagtial. They gained admission to the Campus Ladies' Hostel in their first year of post-graduation. Arun and Vijay, who have been deeply involved in the O. U. Campus for years in the name of research, often encounter new students who greet them warmly and offer their cooperation. They exchange greetings in the morning and evening as they walk through the landscape garden next to the main building of the Arts College.

Professor Lakshmipati, who is a childhood friend of Principal Ramachandraiah, comes now and then on his scooter to walk in the landscape garden on the campus. He greets the students. Principal Ramachandraiah introduced his students Srujana, Deepthi, Arun,

Vijay, and others to Professor Laxmipati over the phone and requested him to take care of them. Arun and Vijay occasionally meet Professor Lakshmipathi during their walks. When Professor Lakshmipathi greets Arun and says, "Arun! Why can't you find a job?" Arun laughs and says, "Sir! Who will give us a job?". Nowadays Arun is working as a reporter for a daily newspaper.

Srujana and Deepti have come to PG final year. Arun is attracted to Srujana. He greets her, taking the initiative. Deepti has observed it. She warns Srujana to be careful.

How fresh and pleasant it would be if four rounds of walking are made in this landscape garden in the morning...! Srujana has started with this feeling. After noticing it two or three times, Arun, who would get up lazily by the time of breakfast, got up quickly at 5:30, got ready, and started for the landscape garden from the Research Scholars' Hostel. Vijay laughed himself, looking at Arun's attitude.

A cold wind blows. Just then the streaks of light emanate in the East. The sun rays are trying to greet the green grass lying on the ground through the alley of the trees, trying to touch the sky.

On one side, some are performing yoga asanas. Some are sitting on the other side and have fallen into some conversation. While walking, Arun looks for Srujana here and there. He slows his pace, not being able to catch up with Srujana, who is briskly walking somewhere. He follows Srujana as she has come fast nearby.

While Arun was following her, he greeted Srujana, saying, "Srujana! There is some meeting on feminism in the Press Club. Your madam is also a speaker along with Olga, Mudiganti Sujata Reddy, and Ratnamala. Shall we go in the evening?"

Srujana laughed and replied, "O.K., elder brother! I will bring Deepti along."

Arun was shocked when she addressed him as "elder brother."

During breakfast, Arun discussed the same matter with Vijay.

Vijay explained to him, "Isn't it common in our Telangana to address elders as elder brother?"

Arun lamented, saying, "Who does he love, if everyone calls him brother...?"

Vijay taught philosophy, saying, "It is a protective shield for women calling men elder brother!"

After listening to the meeting on feminism that evening, Arun felt bored for some reason. As they were leaving the Press Club, Srujana, Deepti, Arun, and Vijay discussed what they had listened to until then while walking by the roadside for the bus number 136.

Arun frankly criticized, saying, "Whatever you say, this feminism and Dalit arguments are nothing but the continuation of the ideological dominance of Andhra people in another form over the people of our Telangana."

Srujana, while laughing, condemned Arun, saying, "It is not like that, brother! What does that have to do with this? Did they oppose the Telangana cause anywhere?"

"You feel the same way. You fall into the trap of Andhra people. If feminism is really what we need, then why did feminism not grow from our Telangana? How well Mudiganti Sujata Reddy and Ratnamala have spoken! They have spoken well about our Telangana society and the limitations of feminism without opposing feminism," said Arun, explaining.

Deepthi said, "It is not like that, brother! How can we think that everything is against us? Are not the BCs and SCs saying that the Telangana movement was born for the upper classes? And are not the leaders of the Telangana movement trying to increase their power by turning towards the BCs, SCs, STs, and Minorities of Andhra and Telangana, breaking the unity among them?"

Arun said, "It is all because of those working in parties like Bahujan Samaj Party deliberately trying to create disharmony among the people of Telangana. In this way, the feminists and the leaders of Dalits of the Andhra region divide the people of Telangana by various names and create disputes among us. They fulfil their leadership, their selfishness, and their interests. Has the Dalit Mahasabha ever cared about the problems of Telangana Dalits? Did it agitate? We ourselves did movements across Telangana with thousands of people in support of Andhra Dalits. Have they done any movement in Andhra in favour of and in support of the Dalits of Telangana? Any caste, in the end, feminism or Dalitism in the region that dominates in development will ultimately be useful to further their dominance. Even though these words are not clearly said, this is the essence of what Sujata Reddy said...!"

Deepti said, "Brother, yours is all male-dominated ideology. You are talking about the patriarchal ideology of upper castes." She further questioned, "Are you not subjected to thought policing like that?"

While they were discussing, the 136 number bus arrived in Hyderguda. However, due to the full rush in it, they left it and resumed their discussion at the bus stop.

"We have to discuss with professors whether it is proper for us to oppose existentialism like that. As part of the Telangana movement, shall we have to follow feminism and Dalitism to develop the movement, leadership, and achieve the demands? Is it possible to take the Telangana movement forward through them? If these are brought forward, will it be possible for everyone to come together? How is unity possible in the movement for Telangana State if these existential arguments are put forward? Didn't Professor Jaya Shankar say these things in the Khairatabad meeting the other day? We have to discuss all these things with Jaishankar sir," said Arun.

"Have not our P.L. Vishweshwara Rao and Simhadri sirs said that we want Telangana while talking about SCs, STs, and BCs and their socio-political empowerment? While saying that Telangana State is necessary for the development of BCs, SCs, STs, and Minorities, the upper castes are developing to some extent in connivance with the people of Andhra. Hasn't it been said many times in the conferences that all the losers are the BCs, SCs, STs, and the Minorities of Telangana?" said Vijay.

Arun said, "Will the BCs, SCs, and STs of Andhra support the BCs, SCs, and STs of Telangana? If they support the Telangana movement, they can be considered genuinely concerned with the people of backward areas, even in feminist and Dalit Bahujan existentialism."

"It is true, elder brother! R. Krishna is not talking about Telangana state fearing that Andhra BCs will leave him. But Naragoni is opposing the Telangana movement. If the BCs and SCs of Andhra leave these leaders if they talk about Telangana, it should be understood that they are accepting their leadership for their selfishness and for their interests. Shouldn't our sociologists and philosophers have argued this point in the meeting held in the Tagore Auditorium?" said Srujana.

"I am not sure. Everything is in confusion," said Arun.

"Why the confusion, elder brother! Aren't people like Mallepally Lakshmaiah, Bellaiah Nayak, B. S. Ramulu, Kanche Ailaiah saying that development is possible only if Telangana state is achieved? Aren't they saying that as the people of Andhra are taking your funds, our water, our coal, our electricity, the Bahujan's of our region are mired in poverty, and they are migrating to Bombay or Dubai due to lack of employment?" said Deepthi.

Just then the 136 number bus arrived. As it was empty, they left in the middle of the discussion and hurriedly boarded the bus.

Madhavi urged Manasa, her son-in-law Sudhakar, Manoj, and Manohar to come for Sankranti. Madhavi asked them to come definitely this time, even if they could not come for Diwali.

From the beginning of the New Year, Sankranthi muggulu were put up all over the town. Various types of food delicacies like snacks and edible preparations made on the occasion of Sankranti, which could be kept for a long time, were being prepared. While walking along the street, one could smell the delicious aroma of frying food delicacies everywhere. As the Sankranti holidays had been declared, there was a bustle of school and college children in the homes.

Madhavi soaked 20 kgs of old rice in water a day before. After removing the water from the rice, the next day morning, she went to the flour mill taking the soaked rice and the maid servant with her. By that time, there was a big line before the flour mill. Madhavi came home and told the maid servant to get the rice milled and bring the flour.

Manasa and Manoj came five days before. Madhavi called again and again as the father-in-law and mother-in-law of her daughter did not come. The next day they also came. Manasa's 'srimantham' was to be celebrated on the day of Sankranti itself. No matter how busy Sudhakar was, he had to come making it convenient. Ramya called from USA and congratulated her. The gifts and bouquets sent online by Ramya have already arrived through courier.

Jaya called over the phone and conveyed congratulations. Despite Manoj's request, Arun, Vijay, Srujana, and Deepthi did not come to his home, citing various reasons. Arun and Vijay stayed in the OU campus.

Discussions are ongoing in various ways about existentialism, a separate state for Telangana, the empowerment of BCs, SCs, STs, and Minorities, the problem of caste, and the problem of leadership.

Arun, Vijay, Srujana, and Deepthi are listening to these discussions and slowly learning about everything. They are discussing and clarifying all matters with Professor Lakshmipati.

"Sir! Anyway, all the arguments seem to divert us from the Telangana movement," said Arun.

"So, what should we do?" asked Lakshmipati with a smile.

He said again, "Everyone has their own problems. It is natural for everyone to want their problem solved first. Therefore, if existentialism, feminism, and the problem of empowerment of BCs, SCs, STs are not paid attention to, it is difficult for all of them to come together in the Telangana movement. Did not Ambedkar also bring the issue of Dalits to the fore and discuss it during the National Movement? He achieved some demands by bringing up the debate on Dalits in the National Movement. When the Congress party opposed the Simon Commission, he invited it and gave a report to it.

He won the communal award and brought reservations into implementation. Gandhi brought Ambedkar with him, saying BCs do not need such a movement. After Independence, even then, the reservations for BCs did not come into effect. So, the problem is not as simple as we think. We should move forward carefully, integrating everything," said Professor Lakshmipathi.

"Sir, whatever it may be, for the development of our region and to become self-sustainable, we require a separate state. It won't be easy for us to grow as long as others dominate our region. Sir, the same sentiment has been expressed multiple times in various seminars," said Arun.

"Nothing can be achieved unless we are determined to take action. It's futile to believe that we were cheated once and will always be deceived. There is only one solution to this problem – we should have our own state. In the seminars held at Osmania University and Delhi, everyone emphasized the regional disparities and the necessity of small states. Even Prime Minister Deva Gouda expressed his support for small states. There must be a separate Telangana," said Arun.

"There have been discussions from different angles, in various places, and among different groups. Ideas, aspirations, and programs may differ, but everyone shares the same goal – the achievement of Telangana state.

Many individuals like Prof. Jaya Shankar, Praja Kavi Kaloji, Dr. Dasarathi Rangacharya, Prof. Biyyala Janardhan, Captain Panduranga Reddy, Venkata Narayana, Prof. Keshav Rao Jadhav, Prof. P.L. Visweswaraiah, Natyakala Prabhakar, Prof. Simhadri, Ambati Surendra Raju, Mallepally Lakshmi, Konda Laxman Babuji, T.N. Sada Lakshmi, etc., have already advocated for our authority over our region. They emphasize the need to develop ourselves, protect our language and culture, ensure that our people get jobs in our region, and have control over our resources. They are mocking our language as not being a language. In the name of language, they said that we are all one and now they say that our language is not understood, and ours' is not at all a language. They are insulting our language by using it for jokers, villains and brokers in movies. They did not come to their senses even though the posters were pelted with stones when they mocked as the people of Hyderabad asked for the sea in a movie. Thus, they are learning many things emotionally and enthusiastically. They are discussing. Thus, arguments in their discussions... Conflict... Professor Lakshmipathi listened to all and explained their root causes.

"Pasham Yadagiri, Nandini Sidda Reddy, Rapolu Anand Bhaskar, Gaddar, B. S. Ramulu, Gade Innaiah, V. Prakash, Nandini Nirmala, Congress MLAs, BJP leaders, Maroju Veeranna, and hundreds of teachers, lecturers, and social activists are conducting seminars in various districts and taluks about separate Telangana," Arun asked doubtfully, "Will Telangana become a reality, sir?"

Lakshmipati responded, "We will achieve it, but a very significant movement has to take place. These conferences, meetings, and seminars are just one phase. You have no idea how massive the movement was in 1969. There needs to be a movement bigger than that. This is possible if the political parties are willing to support it. However, nobody is coming forward. Even the people who have come forward are not heartfully committed to the movement. Everyone is using the Telangana demand for their own interests. The formation of Telangana state is not possible unless a new movement emerges in a different form. If Telangana state is formed, our resources and jobs will be secured, and there will be an increase in respect for our Telangana language and culture. We will have more freedom in making decisions about our region's development, as we discussed earlier."

"Will the movement just come on its own? People do not believe in whoever starts it. They are hesitant because they fear that the leaders will emerge only to drown the movement, as it happened before. The movement will move forward only if a new generation of leadership emerges. Politicians are always seen as cheaters, so the leadership should not be entrusted to them," said Professor Satyanarayana, recalling the past with a bit of rage.

Thus, many things were discussed about the Jai Telangana and the Jai Andhra movements between 1969-72 and their consequences. Commenting on their failure has been done in many ways. They wondered why the movement did not come forward after that.

Professor Lakshmipati reminded, "The sudden rise of the movement started by Jayaprakash Narayan against Indira Gandhi's government at the centre, and the subsequent annulment of Indira Gandhi's election by the court verdict in 1975, which was filed by Raj Narayan stating that the election of Indira Gandhi is invalid, changed all the situations when Indira Gandhi imposed the emergency."

"After the emergency, there was no discussion about the Telangana state, even after changes of governments. The Congress leadership at the center insulted and changed Chief Ministers like Marri Chenna Reddy and Tanguturi Anjaiah in five years in the state. However, in 1982, N. T. Rama Rao and Nadendla Bhaskar Rao brought the Telugu party to power with the slogan of self-respect for Telugu people, erasing everything from people's minds and causing disillusionment."

Thus, the initial discussion led to a conclusion. The formation of Telangana state emerged as the only solution to solve various problems, such as local development, unemployment, construction of irrigation projects, educational development, and the promotion of Telangana language and culture. They arrived at a consensus that resorting to a movement was the need of the hour.

"The backwardness of our region is not due to a lack of resources, as no other region has as many natural resources as ours. The main issue lies in the lack of leadership and the absence of high goals and a comprehensive vision among our people. When our people are given ministerial positions, they tend to agree with whatever the Andhra people say and prioritize their personal interests over the development of our region. There is a fear that not complying with this behaviour may lead to losing their ministerial positions and even jeopardizing their chances of receiving a ticket in the next election. This fear-driven psychology needs to change. Our region can only develop if the mindset of our leaders' changes. Instead of being givers, our leaders have developed a nature of taking. This misery is caused by our dependence on others for survival. While we have imbibed the nature of imparting knowledge, we have not embraced the nature of giving charity. Our people resort to paying penalties and giving bribes."

Do you know one secret? All the subsidies are turning people into receiving nature and reducing them to a dependent psychology of depending on the government."

It is true, sir! They are making everyone dependent on the government and to wait as beggars. I also have to wait for a job after studying so much!" said Arun.

That is not the reason for your problem. Andhra people have already occupied all our jobs in our Telangana. Even if they retire, you may not get jobs. Their children will become local candidates. They are the ones who give... Again, they give jobs to their children. After Telugu Desam Party came into power, Telangana was still devastated". Saying these words Professor Lakshmipati explained as if he is saying something in a new angle.

In room number 57 of the main building at Osmania Campus, a conference was taking place. Srujana, Deepti, and Arun greeted each other. Upon hearing the friendly address of "Hi brother!" used by one of them, some of them couldn't help but laugh inwardly. After the conference, they gathered in groups to discuss the topics presented.

"I really enjoyed reading Olga's novel 'Swechha.' It beautifully depicts the problems faced by women, making us understand the importance of what we truly need and what we might be losing," expressed Srujana.

Deepti chimed in, saying, "I couldn't agree more. 'Ampashayya,' the novel by Warangal Naveen, left a strong impact on me. After reading it, I felt even more compelled to pursue my post-graduation at Osmania Campus."

Srujana said, "That is a male perspective. I did not like it much. I liked the novel 'Swechcha' very well. After the meeting in the Press Club that day, I liked it no matter how much we discussed it."

Vijay said, "I liked the novel 'Bathuku Poru' very much. I felt as if it was written about my mother."

Arun said, "We like one once in a while. Then we may not like it after our status changes. At first, I liked the novel 'Ampashayya' very much. But now all those illusions are gone. That is not my life. But how much I was inspired at first after reading it!"

Srujana said, "I think now you like very much the novels 'Srikanth' and 'Charitraheenulu' written by Sharath Babu. Because Sharath Babu portrayed the characters of Rajeshwari and Srikanth in the novel 'Srikanth' in an unprecedented manner. He portrayed the way of living many lives in one life. He creates sentiments very strongly," she said, laughing.

"I can't even read them now. The mood for reading novels has vanished. Currently, I am engrossed in the works of Vattikota Alwar Swamy, Dasharathi Rangacharya, and Mahidara Ram Mohan Rao. Those novels portray the progress of the movement in those days very well," said Arun.

"Deepti asked, 'Brother! Haven't any novels been written about the Jai Telangana movement of 1969?'"

."I don't know what has been written and what hasn't. Even after pursuing my PG for so many years, I have not landed a single job. I have my own problems," said Arun.

"Sorry, brother! Telangana will surely be achieved. You will also get a job. You will become a professor in this University, and you will be provided canals of irrigation project for your agriculture," said Srujana, smiling.

Deepti smiled, saying, "Let your words come true!"

Arun remained silent, feeling agonized. He said, "What you say will not happen. Our life will end up like this only. We will also die in firing someday, as many died in the 1969 Jai Telangana movement."

The friendship and intimacy between Arun and Srujana grew as they occasionally walked together in the landscape garden of Osmania University. She felt sorry for Arun, who was always on the campus. He didn't seem to go home for any festival. One day, Srujana asked him the same thing.

Srujana asked affectionately, "Brother! Won't your parents wait for you at home?"

"When the stomach is torn, it falls to the feet. The existing agriculture became barren due to the lack of water. My father became indebted as a result of digging borewells repeatedly and committed suicide by drinking pesticide. My mother is working as a labourer. My sister, Thulasi, had to be married with a meagre dowry to brother-in-law Surender, who studied Intermediate. My brother-in-law Surender became indebted as he did not get any work here. So, he went to Muscat and Dubai. My sister Tulasi is maintaining the house with her one-year-old son by making beedis. The money sent by brother-in-law is not enough to pay the debts."

Arun frequently writes small essays for the newspapers. Thus, since Arun is a reporter on the campus, no one questions him why he is staying there. Arun could not bear it as he felt that he was asked why he was staying on the campus though Srujana didn't ask him.

"You don't have any problem, Srujana! Your father is a lecturer. He is sending money every month. What do we have at home? The ultimate destination for a politician is reaching the assembly. But for students and unemployed like us, the OU campus is the ultimate destination." Hopelessness on one hand and sarcasm on the other in Arun's words... Arun is saddened that his life has not changed though so many batches have left.

The darkness was just parting, and the chirping of birds heralded the approaching dawn. Arun woke up with enthusiasm, getting ready for the day. He made his way from the hostel to the landscape garden, walking for quite some time. However, Srujana was nowhere to be seen that day, and the reason for her absence remained unknown. After waiting for an extended period, he returned to his room, only to find that breakfast time had already passed. Vijay informed him that he had received a call from home and proceeded to explain the contents of the conversation.

Arun could not compose himself as he suddenly received a phone call from home, delivering distressing news about his sister Tulasi's life. He was filled with questions about what had happened to his brother-in-law in Dubai. Upon learning about his brother-in-law Surender's death, Arun was in shock and couldn't fathom the cause. Was it murder, suicide, or an accident? The circumstances surrounding his demise remained unknown. Arun did everything within his power to facilitate the repatriation of Surender's body to India, which ultimately took twenty days of relentless efforts.

Surender, Arun's brother-in-law, had sold his land after completing his Intermediate studies to seek employment opportunities in the Gulf countries due to the lack of jobs in their hometown. Meanwhile, Arun's father had accumulated debts while trying to find adequate water for agriculture by digging numerous borewells. The scarcity of power supply for agricultural needs forced his father to resort to pesticide consumption, leading to his untimely demise. Despite objections from Arun's parents, Surender was adamant about pursuing work in Arab countries and left for that purpose. He started sending money back home initially, but communication suddenly ceased after about a year, and attempts to contact him at his reported office number yielded no results.

Arun called Manoj. Manoj's father told Principal Ramchandra and persuaded him to call the MLA. Despite Gangaram's severe efforts, the dead body reached home from Dubai. Sister Tulasi was crying uncontrollably, and a two-year-old boy looked in fear. Arun did not know what to do. Somebody was making preparations for the funeral.

Everyone was expressing words of sympathy, stating that Manoj had not heeded their advice to find livelihood opportunities locally. They recounted the frauds of Gulf agents, the scams in Gulf countries, and the hardships faced there. In front of the house, small firewood sticks and dung cakes were piled up and lit. Someone brought shroud, hallowed rice, incense sticks, and perfume bottles. Another person brought bamboo stalks and was preparing the bier. There was a discussion about bathing the dead body, with some suggesting uncertainty about the duration since death and the condition of the body. Others said it might be enough to sprinkle water on it as it is. There was also concern about who would light the pyre.

The attention shifted to Tulasi's life. It was acknowledged that the one who passed away did so without pain, but Tulasi was not even twenty years old, as one person mentioned. Some present there brought up similar cases seen in other villages. They also mentioned the efforts being made by the Collector, Chief Minister, and the Foreign Embassy to do what they could to help in this situation.

"No matter what you do, nothing will happen. A grown-up son has gone," said the grieving family member.

"Yes, he got his destiny written this much only. It's all his fate," another person replied.

"Which God wrote this destiny! Curses on His temple!" lamented someone else.

"Agriculture is gone. Human beings are thrown into trouble. The lives of those who are alive are disturbed," expressed a saddened individual.

Arun could not control his grief when his mother, his younger sister, and Surender's mother cried, falling on each other. Despite being well-educated, he could not prevent his brother-in-law from going to Arab countries.

No matter how many people they asked, they could not provide employment there. He opened some shop, but it did not work. Arun sobbed as some memories came to his mind.

Manoj, Vijay, and the two other friends from the campus took Arun aside.

Somebody bowed at the feet of the dead body, wrapped in clothes and sprinkled with flowers. Arun followed them and bowed to his brother-in-law for the last time.

Sister Tulasi made her son bow at Surender's feet. She also bowed. Suddenly, she collapsed, bursting into tears.

"How can a mother be holding her son under her arm while lighting the pyre?" There were discussions, different types of discussions, and crying on the other side.

Sister Thulasi took her son under her arm and moved forward, holding the new earthen bowl tightly in a net with the burning fire.

Arun shouldered the dead body in the front row.

The dead body was lifted amidst cries and the slogans of Hara Hara Mahadeva!

After taking two steps, Manoj offered his shoulder. Arun took the fire from his sister Tulasi and held it.

Most of the women stayed at home. The procession of the dead body went ahead.

- Vishalandhra Daily, Ugadi Special Issue, 2017

YOUTHFUL LOVE SPARKS

"Can I love you?"

Someone asked as they stepped towards him. Harika once again posed the same question with a flirtatious smile and sly look. Ashok thought, "Not him." However, she came and sat beside him, repeating the same question while looking into his eyes. Ashok looked back at her, feeling an unknown and indescribable emotion.

The setting was a cool evening on a green lawn with tall trees, creating a cozy and pleasant landscape. The Arts College building shone in the mild sunshine, resembling a gilded magnificent historical edifice. To the west, the Osmania University library building stood tall on an elevated ground, appearing like the pinnacle of knowledge, beckoning to all.

As Ashok continued to gaze at her, she seemed to glow like a nymph amidst the surrounding trees. Suddenly, their eyes met, and both felt an electric sensation coursing through their bodies. Overwhelmed by the moment, Ashok dropped his head and focused on the ground. Harika moved a bit away.

"My name is Harika. I know you. You too might have seen me," Harika smiled mischievously, saying, "Tell me where you have seen me."

Ashok looked at her once again curiously. He recognized her face; it seemed he had seen her several times. He was trying to recollect where he had seen her. He vaguely remembered. She and he met several times in meetings and processions. It seems she has given slogans once or twice. He remembers her making small speeches as well. He recollects one after the other.

Oh! Her name is Harika! He had wanted to know her name many times and what she is studying but he couldn't ask her. Harika appeared surprisingly different today, as if she had come specially prepared for the matchmaking event.

The Harika he saw in processions was different – a strong, passionate woman with clenched fists, shouting slogans emotionally. Was she the same Harika always seen as a heroine in pants, shirts, and Punjabi dress? It appeared she had delicately and beautifully prepared herself for this occasion, making it hard for anyone to recognize her. Ashok couldn't help but admire how beautifully women look when they are well made up. A soft laughter escaped his lips, spreading across his cheeks like a gentle breeze.

"How beautiful you look in this dress!" Ashok complimented her.

"Hmmm! Now you have recognized me! You mean you don't think I look cute in pants and shirts?" Harika asked directly.

"Sorry! That is not what I mean. You look more beautiful in the dress. But that personality and that style are different... This style is different..." replied Ashok.

"Well... now men like you have come to a style of appreciating. Tell me straight at least now... Can I love you?" said Harika and laughed softly.

Ashok laughed while saying, "What is that? Will anyone ask and love? It is like some movie dialogue. What is that question? When did we meet? We do not know each other. There is no friendship between us. How about asking directly if I can love you?"

"It is not like that, you great man! You are in some deep thought. I want to disturb you. I didn't know how to greet you. One will have desires according to one's age. We are at the age of love. Are there other things that are so attractive than love at this age? So, I thought for three days and coined these dialogues and recalled them as a rehearsal in the play as you said. Imagining what your answers will be like, I have also prepared in my mind how I should respond to them."

Ashok asked with a smile, "But did I tell you the answers you expected?"

"It didn't happen so. When I saw you sit like a frustrated lover like Devadas, I thought of bringing you out of your mood. But I don't know your mood. So, the dialogues I expected did not come from your mouth."

Someone came and sat nearby under the shade of the tree. Harika lowered her voice, thinking that they could hear their conversation.

"I thought you would ask me, 'Please don't disturb me. Who are you?' But you responded instantly, like Vishwamitra, who, upon seeing Menaka, got upset, left his penance, and fell in love with her. Thank you."

"But is it all drama? Didn't you genuinely ask?" Harika felt that Ashok was surprised and asked a little crestfallen.

"Ashok! I seriously asked you. I feel I truly want to love you. But I thought if I love you without your permission, it will be one-sided love. One-sided love is a waste. Awareness of life increases. We are working in movements. What is the point of hesitating? Love is also a matter of proper understanding. It is a serious decision that will shape our lives. Therefore, I don't believe in love at first sight. The familiarity, understanding, and friendship that grow through working together and talking together can lead to liking. Liking can gradually turn into love. This is love with real individuality. What do you say?"

Harika felt shy when she noticed that the people talking under the tree turned their heads slightly and looked towards them upon hearing the words "prema, doma."

Soumya came close, waving her hand, saying "Hi Harika"!

"Your dialogue is quite impressive. Tell it once again," Soumya congratulated her and shook her hand, saying, "You have given a wonderful definition of modern love." Harika pretended to be a bit perplexed.

Ashok looked at both in surprise. He turned his gaze and looked up at the top of the tall library building. He felt that the Arts College building seemed to be mocking him with a burst of immense laughter. He doubted whether they were both plotting and teasing him like this. His face scrunched up.

Soumya asked looking at Ashok as if she truly asked as per the plan.

"Harika seems to have feelings for you. You haven't expressed your opinion yet. What do you think, Harika?"

Harika replied, "Why would I ask if I didn't want to love? But this Pravarakhyudu, Sriramachandrudu, talks about everything except love."

Soumya teased Ashok playfully and asked, as if she expected him to answer at least now. "So, does that mean he didn't give you permission to love?"

Ashok hesitated and said, "It doesn't feel right when both of you ask like this. Does anyone really seek permission to love? Shouldn't expressing love come before seeking permission?"

Harika smiled warmly and held Ashok's hand, saying, " That is the actual thing. You're right. That is what I am asking. If you think I'm someone you can love, just tell me, and I'll gladly start loving you."

As Harika's cold hand touched Ashok, he felt something special within him.

"I come from a humble family, and my parents have placed great hopes on me," Ashok said, looking down.

Harika retorted, "Who told you that I come from a rich family? Just because your parents have hopes for you, does that mean mine won't have any hope in me? If we were from a wealthy background, I would be studying engineering or medicine somewhere. Why did I choose to stay on this university campus and in the hostel."

Soumya laughed and added, "Those with some money are heading to the software or medical fields, while the rest of us are like this."

Harika continued the conversation, emphasizing, "In any case, Osmania University is now under the leadership of people from less privileged backgrounds like us."

Soumya noticed that they were drifting away from the main topic of discussion.

Soumya gave a handshake to Ashok, saying, "That is alright, Ashok! It is also my opinion that it is correct nowadays to seek permission like this and love." The three of them laughed gently for some time.

Soumya played the role of mediator, saying, "Harika! Ashok is very shy. It is not appropriate to ask him immediately. Let him think for a few days. If he wants you to love him, he will let you know. What do you say, Ashok?"

Ashok nodded with a positive gesture.

"All right. I am giving you one week. Think. Then only tell me whether I can love you or not. There is no problem in telling Soumya. I will be happy if you love even Soumya." Harika said, "What do you say?" looking at Soumya with a smile.

"The boy is a gentleman. He is pursuing his studies sincerely, and he will earn a job within a short time. His modesty and obedience are good. His body language is also humbly good, like a girl's. Therefore, it would be a happy moment if he says to you, to me, to anybody that you can love me," Soumya said and laughed, making an oblique remark against Ashok, "What type of men are those who, even though at least, can't love themselves, cannot tell those who want to love that they can love?"

Ashok felt as if some electric current passed rapidly through his spine. "It is a fact!" Women think that men are the ones to chase them, that they are in love with them. But it seemed that the two women are teasing him together. Harika said, smiling as if noticing that feeling.

"It is true, Ashok. I honestly want to love you, but you are moody. Maybe there is another lover or imaginary lover in your mind. How do I know? So, I am asking as I thought it better to ask directly and not to make fun of you. We have crossed the teenage. It has been a long time since we have attained the age of loving. Many springs have passed. We fall in love, but we are hesitating in the name of education, movements, employment, caste, and whether parents agree or not," said Harika. She then looked at Soumya and asked, "Am I right, Soumya?"

Soumya gave a short lecture, saying, "Yeah! correct. Nowadays, dowries and castes are playing a major role in love. It's a fact that the youth is falling in love only after knowing their caste also. They want to love only after knowing all the things before to avoid further problems. This problem is not found in any country. They happily express their love for each other in Europe, Japan, America, Russia, or China. They know each other's opinions. They love each other if they wanted to love. Or they leave the love and continue the friendship. In this way, they express opinions with each other through dating and meetings. Parents do not marry their children in those countries. They have to find relationships; they have to love, and they have to get married. If the children say that they love someone and marry, their parents, their relatives, and friends will consider them very humble and respectable children and bless them and marry them. Many people fall in love and get married without even telling their parents and then tell their parents leisurely. There is no issue of dowry and gifts. There is no plight such as searching for in a marriage bureau. All things are discussed and settled together comfortably."

Harika said and certified, "Your lecture is excellent. I have been telling you from the beginning that you will become a good orator and a good lecturer."

Soumya questioned her with fake anger, "Just that! You mean I will not grow up to be a good leader, and I am not suitable to be an MLA or MP? That's it?"

"Who will give you a ticket? If someone comes across an intelligent person, they fear that such a person will outperform them. You will be given a ticket if you learn to be humble and innocent even if you know everything. Till then, you will become a leader for movements, but it is difficult for you to become a political leader and get promoted by others!" Harika expressed her opinion openly.

Ashok belittled them both, saying "So, both of you are political creatures. You are a commodity that wants to grow as a leader through the movement rather than sacrificing for the movement."

At once, both burst out. "Our sacrifices and our struggles are not for others to win as leaders," they flung into an argument like a whirlwind, saying that we alone should grow as political leaders. Some more people came there and joined in the argument. What Harika and Soumya said is very correct. The struggles are ours; the movements are ours, and the leadership is ours. Tomorrow will other people win as leaders in politics. Why should not we win as leaders? When the Jai Telangana movement started in 1969, the activists who carried out the movement emerged as the leaders of that movement. They became political leaders, became MLAs, became Ministers, and became MPs. The current leadership in many fields belongs to those who participated in Jai Telangana and Jai Andhra movements. Why is that sequence not going on now? Why is the bad situation of choosing someone else every time? This false policy must change. The students and youth alone should emerge as leaders in all fields. What do we lack? We lack only money. Are they spending money selling their houses? Aren't that money donations collected by asking someone? Can't we do that? Why shouldn't we become leaders?" Thus, the discussion is going on. Night has fallen. The high max lights are on. No one notices the grass gnats buzzing around. The discussion got heated, and eventually, they got up slowly saying that the message will be closed. They introduced each other and took leave.

Ashok heard the same dialogue repeatedly throughout the night after returning from the mess. The soulful touch of Harika, asking "Can I love you?" while looking into his eyes and placing her hand in his hand, brought him great comfort. The memory of that moment was so reassuring that it made him feel doubly at ease, and he slept peacefully that night after a long time.

Harika and Soumya retired to their respective rooms in the ladies' hostel. Both were lost in their thoughts and couldn't sleep until midnight. Although asking the question seemed easy, after doing so, they felt the weight of its consequences. What if Ashok's answer is negative? How will they bear that shame? They questioned why they had asked in the first place.

Recently, Ashok has been feeling lonely and moody, and this raise concerns that he might be at risk of suicide. Preventing suicides is crucial. Lakshmi Priya argued that people won't contemplate suicide if they believe someone loves them. She shared her own experience of stopping suicide attempts after falling in love, and she even mentioned plans of getting married.

To verify if Lakshmi Priya's statement is true, Harika and Soumya decided to conduct an experiment. Nobody knows it. For the first time, they felt that they were stuck in another thing else as a result of the thought of doing something. They weren't sure what was lacking in Ashok to love him, but they convinced themselves that their actions were not wrong.

After completing her morning bath, Harika entered the breakfast section in the mess and searched for Soumya. It appeared that Soumya was also seeking Harika. They greeted each other with a warm "hi" and moved to a corner to discuss whether their actions from the previous day were morally justified.

Soumya supported Harika, stating, "I think we haven't done anything wrong. Those who can't experience love or don't have the opportunity to love may resort to suicide. Suicides decrease when people believe there's at least one person who loves them. Let's discuss this with Professor Laxman in the afternoon."

Harika disagreed, saying, "No, even those who have loved someone might consider suicide if their love fails. Don't you agree with me?"

Soumya responded, "Alright, we'll meet with the professor in the afternoon and discuss this further." After concluding their discussion, they both headed back to the tiffin section.

In the afternoon, they walked towards the office of Professor Lakshman in the Art College, who always advises them in the movement. They explained their feelings about what happened.

Lakshman laughed, saying, "You are too late," and shared his experiences. Just then, his wife Srujana, an Assistant Professor, came in smiling and sat down. Lakshman introduced Harika and Soumya to Srujana.

"Yes. As Lakshman said, you are too late. We studied at this University. Similarly, then we participated actively in the students' movements. A few hundred students fell in love and got married as part of that movement. Our wedding also similarly took place. Like you, I took the initiative then," Srujana laughed, saying, "He is the same in those days and now."

Lakshman said, "Harika! She is upper caste, but I am lower caste. I am an introvert, and I fear telling them I love her. It doesn't bother her though. She takes pride in her upper caste identity and considers it self-confidence. She took the initiative in our relationship, but that doesn't mean she was the first one to love me, and I didn't love her."

Srujana, an Assistant Professor, expressed, "Harika! Even after many years of marriage and with our children studying in college, he still mocks me, labelling me as an arrogant upper caste. If we don't conform to their expectations, their egos get hurt, and they attribute it to caste arrogance. The concept of feminism came into play, and we believe in gender equality, so I think men should equally share the responsibilities. I question why I have to make tea for him every time, and he responds with his male chauvinism, associating it with my caste." Srujana laughed and added, "If given the chance, he only uses it to curse my caste of birth."

"Harika! They came into the movement during that time and participated actively more than us. We thought it was all a great adventure." Professor Lakshman said, looking at Sujana with a smile, as if questioning whether it was true or not. He continued, "But it is not known until somebody said in those days that these women are joining the movement just to marry the men they liked without dowry."

"Is it a blunder to come into the movement thinking in that way? Is that wrong? Who can't help but love seeing young people coming forward with a great understanding of society and dedicating their lives to change this society drastically?" Srujana replied.

"Don't get so angry. I said it as a joke. Take it lightly. In any country, thousands of people fell in love and got married when movements took place. Finally, many people fell in love and got married even in wars where they were alert from moment to moment. That is a natural order too. The strangest thing is that even though this new movement has been going on for a long time now, no one said, except you, sir, 'we like each other, help our marriage.' That too to ask if we can love, sir! I don't know whether society is going forward or going back. We made love comfortably before you were born. We built movements. We never considered anything contradictory to each other. But whatever task you undertake, you do it blindly. However, the best of the bad of a lot." He looked directly into their eyes while smiling and asked, "But are you ready to love Ashok?"

Srujana supported them, saying, "How can girls say more clearly than this? How great you are!"

"It is true, madam! I honestly want to love Ashok. But in the environment where we grew up in our village, loving is not a part of our life. Unless society changes a lot, love does not seem to be a part of life in our region. This is a system where people are getting married only after taking into consideration caste, religion, parents, brothers, property, and status. This is a male-dominated system that looks down on a girl as a weakness if she says she is in love. That is why, though I want to love, I am unable to love. If boys come after us saying that they love us, we don't feel like believing them. This is a state of dilemma, sir." Thus, Harika spoke openly to the Srujana and Laxman couple. Similarly, Soumya also explained her experiences.

Srujana went into the memories of those days, saying, "So do you mean we haven't experienced all these in our time? Do you think there would have been an egalitarian society then? The system was much worse than this. Now it has changed a lot. Now if the children say that they are in love, the parents are getting their children married, though the boy or girl is inter-caste. After the advent of family planning, as the offspring is one or two, no one can leave them. In our case, the people from my side and his side did not talk to us properly for two years after our marriage. They spoke to us after I gave birth to their grandson." Her best friend Swarnalatha went into the movement to radically change this society, to build an egalitarian society, and to bring a new democratic revolution. We never met again after that. I couldn't see at least her dead body at last. How many times did she think of seeing Swarnalatha? How excited she was to join a movement like Swarnalatha! Where have gone today the lofty goals, passions, and sacrifices of the youth of those days...? All the friends of the movement were scattered somewhere. A layer of tears formed in Srujana's eyes.

Professor Lakshman said, as if he noticed Srurjana's thoughts and anxiety, "Srujana, society seems to be going backward in some respects. Sacrifice is the calling of the age of those days. It was the time when people yearned to make sacrifices to do their best in the evolution of society rather than pursuing their bright future. The issues of property and status, which did not exist in those days, have now greatly increased. Do you deny?" said Professor Laxman.

Professor Laxman turned to Harika and Soumya and said, "But it is not just a problem related to both of you. It's not limited to you only. It's not limited to our region only. It's a problem faced by millions of youths in our country. This is not a problem to be solved in isolation. It is an issue linked to the total society, the values of culture, the system of family, and the system of caste." Thus, he explained for a long time. They assured them that they would have the moral support of both of them, telling them to move forward as they are doing the right thing.

Ashok too had the same doubt. Ashok met two more friends, and they talked together. Not knowing anything, both of them also met Professor Daya Sagar. They asked, as if they were discussing some theory rather than their problem. After hearing everything, Professor Daya Sagar sympathized and explained it well.

A classmate of ours used to say, reciting poetry to everyone, "Youthful age calls to love someone. The social movements excite people to make sacrifices for the sake of society and the nation. Finally, even life should be sacrificed for it." That word inspired many people. Many fell in love while participating in the movement. They got married. Ours is also a love marriage. The call of the youthful age is of two types. One is love, and the other is sacrifice. In any generation, the new young generation is eager to make sacrifices for society. The youthful age calls for mutual love when there is no such environment.

But movements make it natural to love as well as sacrifice. However, the present situation is going differently. This is the tragedy. Movement generally increases courage and collective dynamism. That is the real movement. But suicides have increased in this movement like never before. When the emotion and excitement have grown to a stage intending to do something for society and social change, and when the thought of making a sacrifice constantly urges a person, and if the leadership is not able to give a proper program for it, the emotion and sacrifice will flow in reverse into frustration. At this stage, they are tempted to think that the sacrifice of their life will be useful for carrying the movement forward. This is all about the topic related to social psychology. Some sadists are saying that it is mass hysteria. They are idiots and anti-movement. The people who say that those who sacrificed their lives are cowards are the ones who are stupid. It is a fact that they are cowards. Those who have guts will courageously get involved in militant movements for the sake of the movement, but they will not talk lightly about the sacrifices of other people's lives. Thus, Daya Sagar analyzed many things and said, "I want you to grow up to be good leaders."

Harika is waiting for Ashok's decision. Ashok is waiting for Harika's decision and opening a conversation with her. Days passed without deciding who to open a conversation at first. Soumya is angry.

Soumya flared up, saying, "This time I will not come as a mediator. What kind of human beings are you who can't even express love like utter stupid and cowards?" Soumya said, "Tata bye-bye" and left, laughing, saying, "You go to hell. How you express your love is up to you. Don't ask me once again." Since then, Soumya has been avoiding Harika.

On that day, the students were discussing something under the trees in front of Arts College. Some were suggesting that everyone should go to Lakshmi Priya's wedding together and have a grand celebration.

Under a tent at the steps of Arts College, someone was giving a speech to the students at the hunger strike camp. Some others were shouting slogans, raising their fists.

Coming from the University library towards Arts College, Soumya saw Harika under the trees and walked towards her, thinking that it had been many days since they met. Harika was looking towards the hunger strike camp, and Soumya focused on the direction Harika was looking. Ashok was seen among the public, shouting slogans.

Soumya approached Harika and asked, "Hi Harika! What about your love? How long will you have to wait?"

"He will come to us after withdrawing his hunger strike at the hunger strike camp today," said Harika with confidence.

"Did you cast any spell? Have you tried hypnotism? How sure are you?" Soumya inquired.

Harika behaved in a reserved manner and said, "I know."

Dusk was spreading, and it was getting dark under the trees. Many students were leaving from under the trees, but only a few remained. Harika and Soumya were waiting, desperately looking to leave.

As they expected, Ashok greeted them with a smile, saying, "Hi Harika! Can I love you?"

Soumya congratulated Ashok and Harika, saying, "This reverse dialogue ends so wonderfully. Congratulations!"

"But Soumya, don't tell anyone about this until we tell you. You should declare yourself in Lakshmi Priya's marriage," said Harika.

Vartha Daily, Sunday Edition,2011

NEW! EVERYTHING IS ENTIRELY NEW!
Telangana: Embracing Change and knowledge.

The rainy season has arrived.

The trees have turned lush green as the rain has washed away the dust from their leaves. As part of the Haritha Haram, new saplings are being planted all around.

In Krishna Nagar, Jagtial, a new house is buzzing with the excitement of a wedding. Krishnaveni has just finished getting ready and is about to leave on her scooty. She has received a marriage proposal recently, and the prospective groom's family is expected to visit either tomorrow or the day after.

Gangadevi, who is just coming home, asked Krishnaveni, "Where are you going?"

Gangadevi herself is busy preparing for the Groups with the announcement from the Telangana Public Service Commission.

Krishnaveni is waiting eagerly for the announcement to fill up vacant teacher posts in ZP. She had been selected in the last round, but the appointment orders are yet to be issued. There is news that DSC will be held again.

Krishnaveni replied to Gangadevi's question, counter-questioning, "Where are you going?"

After the formation of our Telangana, books have changed. New things are now being known about our new state. We will only pass in the Groups if we study all these books. All these years, we have been made ignorant of our history. Ours is a new state with a new history, and many books have been written about our culture and past. We plan to buy some of these books, but unfortunately, not all of them are available in Jagtial.

Krishnaveni parked her scooter using the side stand and entered the house, saying, "You are right!" All the textbooks have been changed starting from the first class. I have gone through the new textbooks to prepare for the DSC. I wonder how many new things there in the Telugu textbook are! We must read those books first; only then we will realize how much more we need to learn to educate our students.

"I have just had my breakfast. Today, Mother has prepared idli, so I don't need tea. It is getting late; let us go!"

"Where shall we go?" asked Krishnaveni.

Krishnaveni and Gangadevi have been classmates since childhood. They move together like a couple of poets and sisters, thanks to Krishnaveni's scooty. Recently, Krishnaveni's family built a terraced house on the plot they had purchased long ago. On the other hand, Gangadevi's house, located in Krishna Nagar, has become old, and the road has been raised high, making the house look low-lying. It is an old tiles house that was built before others started constructing houses when the agricultural fields were converted into plots. In those days, it was great to build such a house, but now it looks like a house of the very poor.

In the inner hall, Krishnaveni's mother is tying the beedies, which are arranged in the winnowing basket, into bundles. On one side of the winnowing basket, some tobacco is seen.

"Gangadevi greeted her by asking, 'Aunty! Has uncle already left for school?'"

"He took the meals box and left on the bike fifteen minutes ago as it was already late. Don't you know that he puts his bike in the bus stand and goes to Dharmaram by bus?" replied Venkatamma.

Gangadevi observed the entire house as it shone brightly on a 200-yard plot, surrounded by a compound wall with a fine lappam finish. Some people criticized the timing of constructing the house during Krishnaveni's marriage. They wondered how long

Krishnaveni's family would stay on rent and who would marry her if they continued to live in a rented house. Nowadays, boys also seek their mother-in-law's house to be beautiful.

Krishnaveni's father, Lakshmaiah, initiated the construction of the house after understanding that a girl's marriage prospects improve when she possesses a perfect combination of education, beauty, height, a handsome dowry, a specific caste, and good manners. Lakshmaiah has sought some alliances for Krishnaveni, but they did not proceed further due to the family's lack of their own house. Instead, they made some lame excuses without directly expressing their concerns.

Nonetheless, Lakshmaiah managed to complete the house by borrowing some loans. The resulting two-bedroom independent house is now a beautiful abode, attracting marriage proposals after its construction.

"It has been ten days since our washerwoman has not come. They do not come, and they don't allow others to come. I don't understand what this caste binding is all about. Though we have built a new house, the old castes are not disappearing. After going there, go to the washerwoman's house," said Venkatamma.

Venkatamma hurried them, saying, "Start immediately. If you are late, the washerwoman will go to someone else's house."

Krishnaveni started the scooty, and Gangadevi sat in the back seat.

They are going on the scooty from Krishna Nagar via Angadi Bazar. Anisette Prabhakar's statue was seen in the Angadi.

Alishetti Prabhakar was a great poet. It was thought of installing his statue for so many years, but no writer had taken the initiative. Finally, the Association of Photographers took the initiative and installed the statue, claiming that 'Alishetti Prabhakar is our photographer,' said Krishnaveni.

"Alishetti Prabhakar's poem has been prescribed in the Telangana textbook. Similarly, a lesson about Muddu Rama Krishnaiah, who retired in 1965 as the Headmaster of our

Multipurpose High School, Jagtial, has also been prescribed. But a lesson about the poet, Ramasimha, has not been prescribed. It would have been better if it were prescribed. Everything is new. It seems that they are not aware of the poet Ramasimha," said Gangadevi.

"I think Alishetti Prabhakar's statue is the first among the writers of our district," said Krishnaveni.

Gangadevi, who was preparing for the competitive exams, said, "No," and remembered what she had read.

"A temple was built for the poet Ramasimha in Raghavapatnam of Sikhs near Gollapalli. It is just 15 km away from Jagtial. It is said that he lived for 125 years. He used to go like Shivaji on a horse, holding a sword, before the fort of feudal lords and sing his poems and songs! It is said that 100 years ago, on learning that the poet Ramasimha was coming, the feudal lords used to lock their forts and run away because they were so afraid! It is said that people listened to his songs and poems enthusiastically. He used to sing the songs of "Who is the feudal lord... (Dora evadura...) The land belongs to the tiller... (Dunne vadide Bhoomi...); he did more after he was imprisoned and released from jail. People built a temple for him after his death. K.V. Narendra wrote an interesting article about the poet Ramasimha in the magazine," said Gangadevi.

The scooty goes past Angadi Bazar, from Tehsil Chowrasta, through Mochi Bazar, and past the vegetable market through the clock tower. When someone greeted them, they said hi and moved forward without stopping. The scooty turned left from Laddu Khawaja Chowrasta and took a turn towards Washerman Street.

The washerwoman, Pavani, was just about to leave the house. Upon seeing Krishnaveni, Pavani smiled at her as a greeting and stopped. Pavani is two years older than Krishnaveni. She spoke as if she had grown up a lot. She has two children.

"It has been ten days since you haven't come. Mother is shouting," Krishnaveni said.

Pavani smiled and replied, "I had a fever."

Krishnaveni laughed and said, "You are looking good! Did you get a fever? You are leaving to go to someone's house. Mother said that if you don't come twice a week, you will be discontinued."

Pavani, who studied in 7th class, also irons clothes. Her husband is a leader in the Rajaka Association. When Pavani thought of quitting this washing job, her mother-in-law continuously pestered her son and took four houses in the auction of Rajaka Association to wash clothes, paying twenty thousand rupees to the Association. Pavani expressed this with indignation. Meanwhile, Pavani's children were playing in the street.

Pavani laughed and said, "You can discontinue. We took your house in the auction, paying five thousand rupees to the Association. We will give your house to whoever pays the interest. Hire someone who washes clothes well. My mother-in-law is bedridden, and I cannot cope with two children. I will set up a shop to iron starched sarees."

The mother-in-law, who was in bed at home, flared up in anger. She reproached her daughter-in-law, saying, "How did we survive all these years if we didn't wash clothes to survive? Today you have become fashionable. Don't we get a marriage gift if this Kittava gets married?"

"We worshipped Goddess Pochamma the day before yesterday. We celebrated the occasion in the trees," said Pavani as an explanation.

"Despite saying two days, she went to her mother's house for five days," the mother-in-law complained. She sat up from the bed.

Pavani smiled and said, "I have left for your home only today."

"You say you have left for our house because I have come to your house. I have left for washing all the good dresses. There are many clothes of the mother. At least two should be washed at home. After I get a job, I will buy a good washing machine. Hu." Said Krishnaveni and started the scooty.

Pavani smiled and asked, "Is anybody coming to visit and look over a prospective bride?"

They went ahead with the scooty, saying, "Yes, let's leave early."

While coming, Gangadevi looked at the bookshops in the Clock Tower Circle. The shops were just being opened.

Gangadevi went to two shops and bought some guides and books.

Gangadevi said, "Still, we have to search for books related to Mission Bhagiratha, Mission Kakatiya, double-bedroom houses for the poor, tap connections for every house, the Chief Minister KCR's PowerPoint presentation about irrigation projects, Hyderabad as 'Viswanagaram,' IT, and startup. Let's go towards the shops in the old bus stand," said Gangadevi.

"It is said six and a half lakh people are writing! There are not even six or seven hundred posts. Why so much effort? What a waste of time," said Krishnaveni.

An elderly person intervened in the conversation, saying, "If everybody thinks like that, who will write the examinations? Who will get the jobs? Who will buy all these guides and books? When will you learn about our Telangana? If you don't know while writing the examination for employment, when will you know?"

Gangadevi looked at him and recognized him as Shankaraiah, the retired Principal of Degree College. Both of them greeted him, saying "Namaskaram, sir!"

Principal Shankaraiah looked at them, smiling, and said, "We have achieved our Telangana. You don't know how many movements we have participated in since 1968 for the formation of this Telangana state. It is essential to know about it, especially when preparing for competitive exams. Understanding our history is crucial."

Krishnaveni nodded in agreement, indicating that what he said was true.

The retired Principal Shankaraiah suggested, "Rajesham, the Lecturer, gives excellent guidance regarding the preparation for the

Groups exam. He will recommend the relevant books for you to read."

After paying the bill, the two of them left, saying, "We agree with you."

"Everything is entirely new, and yet we have to study hard. The entire syllabus has been changed, and we are unsure how much history it covers. The Telangana Public Service Commission has prescribed this syllabus for all the examinations, which is a positive thing. It's essential for you to study too, as it will improve your general knowledge," Gangadevi advised.

Scooty turned to the North from the Clock Tower. It passed the Geeta Bhavan and the Merchants Association Building, then turned right and headed East. They took one or two books from the Book Stall near the old bus stand and proceeded towards the old bus stand. They went to the Jagtial Municipal Office, paid the water bill, and got out.

"Let us meet Lecturer Rajesham sir now," said Gangadevi. The scooter proceeded to Dharmapuri Road from the old bus stand.

The trees have been providing cool shade at the Women's Degree College for decades. The students of the college are planting saplings inside the compound wall. Krishnaveni and Gangadevi walked towards the staff room.

After meeting Rajesham sir, they came out gathering some information from him.

"We have a lot of history that we need to know... You also study," said Gangadevi when Krishnaveni was about to start the scooty.

"I will think when DSC is announced... We are not sure whether there will be DSC or not until new districts are formed and everything is settled! How will the DSC syllabus be then?" said Krishnaveni.

"What if the DSC is held anytime? Where does the knowledge you gained go? All this must be read for teacher posts also. It is said that at last for police jobs as well, the syllabus about the whole of Telangana has been prescribed," said Gangadevi.

Next to the old bus stand, the statue of Headmaster Muddu Ramakrishna, which was installed five years ago on the occasion of the centenary of the Old High School, is seen upright as if it is blessing everyone from the other side of the short compound wall. While they are passing the bus stand and passing through Tehsil Chowrasta, there is a procession of students coming from somewhere.

Seeing the enthusiasm of the students in the Haritha Haram procession, Krishnaveni is thrilled when she will get a job as a teacher. She has stopped the scooty and stood there for a while.

-21 August 2016; Namaste Telangana

OH, MY DEAR! I AM COMING!

Would you like me to write about that today? What should I write about? Back in those days, I didn't understand the true meaning of friendship. Was it really friendship? Do you recall those days? There was no electricity. There were no tar roads or synthetic fabrics. People wore handloom cotton clothes. There was no ironing. There were no terraced houses. Vehicles like cars, buses, and bikes were few and far between. Transportation was mainly done on bullock carts or by walking. Roads were often made of metal and gravel, sometimes just footpaths or bullock cart tracks. I didn't wear shoes, and many times, my toenails would bleed from stepping on stones. I remember my father applying turmeric and using old cloth as a makeshift bandage for those wounds.

Waking up before dawn and cleaning teeth using charcoal, drawing water from a well with a bucket, and pouring water quickly over the head—these were the activities. Lalita used to compete with us.

Occasionally, we would go for a bath to the agricultural field at the diesel pump, Dunkin. We would pluck neem twigs on the way and chew on them while walking. Do you recall the striped underwear made from Binni cloth?

We escaped from the danger of water multiple times by going swimming and avoiding Lalitha. On that particular day, we were swimming in the Mothe village pond, competing to swim from one side to the other. As I struggled in the water, feeling short of breath and on the verge of drowning, someone quickly came to my rescue, pulling me to the shore. The memory of that incident is accompanied by the vivid recollection of my mother's stern scolding and severe beating. Those were the times we often hurt ourselves while learning to ride a bicycle.

During my childhood, it was often mentioned that Lalitha would be my wife, and this thought filled me with happiness. Right from our early days, I playfully teased her. Whenever tears welled up in her eyes, a sense of pity would overcome me. I indulged in various tricks and antics to bring smiles to her face and ensure her happiness. I distinctly recall the instance when, on the banks of a large irrigation well, I went to gather a caldera flower for Lalitha and a water snake suddenly coiled around my leg. Do you still remember that incident?

How many lotus flowers were in the moat built around Jagtial Fort? I wanted to bring and give some to Lalitha. I hoped to go down the stairs next to the main gate of the fort and pluck lotus flowers. I feared the idea of dying with lotus vines coiled around me. Once someone plucked a lotus and gave it to me, I felt proud, as if I had plucked it myself. I thought about boasting to Lalitha about it. I wondered how buffaloes managed to come down the stairs of the difficult tunnel into the ditch. It was amazing. The smell of ammunition lingered in the ammunition warehouse of Jagtial Fort. The place was pitch dark, and everything inside was dusty. I had hoped to find some iron shells there. I had thoughts of playing with Lalitha using those iron shells.

When it was announced that Lalitha had grown up and reached puberty, I remember making her sit in a corner. I was told not to touch her while I measured and saw that she was only the length of four fingers shorter than me. She was offered soaked rice and copra, and everything was meant for her. It was said that men should not eat those things, as consuming them would hinder the growth of a moustache. They didn't allow us to have those things because of this reason. Lalitha, who used to wear a short skirt and jacket every day, suddenly wore a saree on that day. Food was served to everyone, and when she was made to wear the saree, it seemed like she had grown up significantly. From that point on, she stopped playing with us.

All the games that we played with Lalitha have come to a halt. We used to engage in activities like tiger and goat, playing cards with empty cigarette boxes, and indoor games such as 'punjeetham', 'pacheesu' using seashells, and 'badhi' with tamarind seeds. We would run around with twirlers made of palm leaves. We would attempt to catch small, winged insects like dragonflies with wings during the rainy season. When red insects and cochineals resembled pearls, we collected them in matchboxes, carefully placing them in our pockets, and our hearts would fill with delight upon seeing them. Lalitha, you, and I ventured to harvest tiny plums from the agricultural fields, despite getting scratches on our hands and feet, tearing our shirts. The fear of Mother's scolding loomed over us, and we would return home after darkness had fallen.

Even subsequent to that time, Lalitha and I would covertly pluck rosary peas from the fences of gardens and bring them along. The rosary peas, shining in hues of red and slight black, were remarkably bright. The sound of water emanating from the sluice of the tank held us captivated. The water in the agricultural wells contained moss and weeds, and the canal water was muddy. The experience of fishing with our hands in the canal water was truly exceptional. We would feel the baby catfish nibbling at our hands.

After that, Lalitha stopped coming to school as well. She got married within a year and was sent to her mother-in-law's house. Lalitha was no longer my wife. Does everything one thought as a child would happen? Mother consoled me. Why did she get married before...? I asked my mother why they wouldn't marry me, and she laughed. At that time, I was in the 10th class. She said, "Get a moustache on your face, and I will find you a more beautiful girl." Thus, Lalitha got away. She became pregnant before two years had passed. She came home for delivery. When I met her then, I was amazed at how maturely she spoke and how much she had grown in a year. Unfortunately, both the mother and child died due to labour pains. They said it was tetanus and that the foetus had turned transversely. Thus, Lalitha left, leaving behind memories.

On the day of Ugadi, when my mother was exultant, she put a garland made of sugared birds and copra around our necks. We were eager to bite into them. Lalitha would ridicule us, asking whether men eat copra. You, Lalitha, and I always waited for relatives to come. If the relatives came, there would be chicken, and at least the egg would be cooked. On that day, rice would be prepared instead of maize. When relatives came, they would bring bananas. Do you remember waiting for the relatives to come over for bananas? After coming from school, we would sprinkle jowar while the chickens gathered around, making clucking sounds.

We used to go on foot, carrying luggage, when we journeyed from Jagtial to Kondagattu or Vemulawada. Wherever we went, Lalitha followed us, saying she would come along. She would run ahead of everyone else, ensuring that no one could catch her. During these walks, I often experienced pain in my legs. I would walk alongside my grandfather, grandmother, father, mother, elder brother, and elder sister. If I complained about my legs aching, my father would hoist me onto his shoulder and carry me for a while. Do you recall those moments?

We used to embark on trips from Jagtial to the Yellamma temple in Vellulla, near Metpally, and to Dharmapuri, where we would take a sacred bath in the Godavari River. We would carry rice, pulses, and utensils, all bundled together. The fatigue from walking was undeniable, yet it was intertwined with a sense of satisfaction. The smiles on our faces, although faded, served as ornaments in our lives. Despite the challenges, those days were filled with numerous joys. Our hearts flourished amidst the lush green surroundings. The trees, the birds, and their melodious chirping-what a soothing and delightful natural orchestra! The harmonious symphony of insects in the forest was equally sweet and comforting. The essence of the day revolved around the bonds of friendship.

Can you recollect that particular day? During our journey on foot to my grandmother's village, we encountered a field of groundnuts. We uprooted some and greedily consumed the raw nuts, driven by hunger. Unfortunately, this impulsive act led to a bout of dizziness due to biliousness, causing us to fall.

One memory etched into my mind is that of my grandfather igniting his cigar using a flintstone. The image is indelible. I still marvel at the coarse dhoti he used to wear. The intricate way in which he draped an eight-cubit turban around his head remains a wonder. He would tuck his cigar into the folds of his turban, and a towel rested on his shoulder. Buttons were fashioned from cloth, exemplifying the simplicity of those times.

In my grandmother's village, when a girl strolled along the embankment of the Jowar fields, we playfully whistled and then quickly hide amidst the Jowar fields. Oh, how vividly do I recall... Do you remember that innocent, joyful expression on the face of the village girl? She glanced around, her eyes brimming with curiosity, and upon finding no one around, she too broke into a gentle whistle. A sweet smile graced her lips as she glanced about one last time before continuing on her way. Wasn't her name Susheela?

Oh, the memories flood back – the fields we explored together, Susheela! The countless heart-to-heart conversations we shared, echoing with laughter. The flavors of our adventures were as rich as the roasted ears of maize with their husk and fibrous silk. Remember the joy of shaking the grains of jowar from the roasted heads? And how we would prepare cow gram in a pot, carefully layering it with castor leaves, turning it upside down, and letting the fire weave its magic around it? The taste of steamed cow gram was a symphony of delight. Let's not forget the incredible taste of freshly baked raw groundnuts. How many conversations did Susheela engage us in? It was for her that we enthusiastically participated in the 'Binaca Geet Mala' competition on Radio Ceylon, writing cards to request songs for the listeners. How many letters did we draft for All India Radio urging them to broadcast the songs we yearned for?

Recollections come flooding in of the 50-kilometer dual bicycle journey from Jagtial to Karimnagar that we embarked upon. Our rented bicycles carried us on a joyful adventure. And what an evening it would become – two movies to enthral us! In those bygone days, after the curtains closed on the second screening, we would quench our thirst and rest at the bus stand, lulled into slumber, only to set off back to Jagtial before the break of dawn. How well I remember the fever that coursed through our bodies due to the swollen calves resulting from our bicycling escapades. For three days we lay bedridden, and when our parents inquired about the cause, we tactfully evaded the truth, muttering that it was nothing to be concerned about.

When grandmother was spinning the Khadi thread, we used to sit there, listening to the brilliant music. We got mesmerized by listening to Dudekula Saheb's bow, which was cleaning cotton and releasing so much cotton and dust into our noses, mouths, and heads. After hearing the stories of our lies, Mother gave us two blows. Father set a condition to buy new clothes for Dussehra...! When we wanted to study by the light of a kerosene lantern, our parents would put out the lantern and provide a small dim kerosene lamp without a glass chimney because the lantern consumed more kerosene! We would fall asleep while studying in a lying position in the mud house on the pial. When we blew our noses in the morning, it was all soot...!

I used to pick up fallen raw mangoes in the mango groves and eat them so much that my nose and mouth became sore from their juice...! Once, I had a stomachache and cried for two days after eating some unripe fruit. My mother stayed with me, straining her eyes without sleep...!

Do you remember the time when I ran away from home because my father had beaten me...? It took three hours to walk to my maternal aunt's house. The bus fare was 30 paise, but we could save 30 paise if we walked...! Whenever our mother asked us to visit our maternal aunt's house, we would walk for the trip there to save money, and then we'd return by bus. Do you remember watching the Lava Kusa movie at Jawahar Talkies for 28 paise and sitting on the sand after buying a floor ticket?

In the past, my grandfather used to hide all the rolls of thread to weave a blanket, while my grandmother was spinning Khadi rolls of thread. My grandmother used to fuss that she should give them away at the Khadi production centre.

During the rainy season, we would go up into the trees and celebrate Pochamma, Yellamma, and Bonalu festivals. It was a wonderful experience to hold the top in the palms of our hands while it was spinning on the ground. Lalitha looked at it with surprise! Sushila used to spin the top longer than any of us. Do you remember when Satyam broke his leg because the branch of a tree, he was sitting on snapped during the game of 'kothi komma,' a children's play? I almost hurt my back when I fell while cutting the tender leaves of the tamarind tree. We used to eat raw tamarind and make others' mouths water.

How far did we walk in search of jamun fruits along the Nizamabad Road? How far did we go to find the flame of the forest tree for its leaves, which we stitched together to make eating plates? After walking to collect firewood, we gathered and brought back dried small sticks. We were so scared when we saw red and black scorpions and had to walk close to them. We even collected dried dung cakes! Mother used to follow the cattle herd and gather the dung, bring the rice husks, mix them, and make dung cakes. After beating them against the wall, she would preserve them once they were dry. Lalitha and I competed in everything!

When I asked my father to buy crackers for Diwali, he said there was no money. So, we decided to find an alternative way to experience the joy of burning firecrackers. We filled a small iron container with potash and struck it against the wall, simulating the sound and excitement of firecrackers. The arrival of electric lights in our village brought immense happiness. It felt like witnessing the grandeur of Indra's heavenly abode in movies.

New Desires (Modern Short Stories)

Some of our friends discontinued their education and went to Bombay in search of work. Those who didn't pass their 12th-grade exams at Multipurpose High School in Jagtial also stopped pursuing further studies. Ibrahim chose to run a Pan Shop, while Buchiramulu found employment in a cloth shop. Venkat Narayana secured a temporary position as a chief mason in Darur Camp, and Shankar became an RTC Conductor.

It was Rakhi Pournami Day when an unexpected visitor, Susheela, arrived. She tied a Rakhi around my wrist, affectionately calling me her elder brother.

It feels good to have childhood again. However, childhood isn't solely about joy; it also encompasses hardships and tears, underscoring the complexity of life.

Raja Ram's life became immensely challenging after his mother passed away and his father was left to care for him. His father used to go to work. Cooking was difficult for them. Consequently, Raja Ram dropped out of school to contribute to the family's welfare. Similarly, Satyam faced difficulties after his father's demise, and his mother had to work as a labourer to sustain the family. Satyam's inability to afford a school uniform led to him standing in the sun outside the classroom for days. His mother endured hunger and slept on an empty stomach. They faced financial constraints and struggled to find work opportunities. Securing a government job became a significant aspiration, even if it seemed unattainable. The pursuit of such a position was akin to chasing a distant and elusive goal.

Our friendship has not broken. Our friendship has not faded. The feelings are still lively. It is like a fixed deposit made in the bank. Memories may bring more happiness to life than the present. So, what did Krishna Swami say when he was asked to write about hardships? Did he refuse to write?

Why do we write about tears? Did he say that when the goal is to reach our objective, we should talk about the comforts and honors received, as well as the destination we reached? Why should we withhold insults, tears, and hardships? Yes, that is also true.

My beloved! The reactions, sensations, and feelings are fading. They are drying up. Similar to how this body ages, experiences turn into sensations, sensations transform into memories, and even memories decay and fade away. The body is displaying wrinkles. Old age stands before us like a tiger.

Nature remains unchanged. Living beings stay the same. The sea retains its timeless nature. The rivers continue to flow as usual. Likewise, the rains still fall. The Himalayas radiate their enduring brilliance. Trees bear fruit without alteration. Cattle, chickens, and birds are born and grow just as they always have. Nature persists perpetually. The lives of birds continue their uninterrupted rhythm. Are we the ones who have changed? Are we the ones undergoing change?

A tree leaves no traces of itself. For thousands of years, nature and livestock have continued to exist, and none of them are out of order. Their journey continues. You and I are on the same journey.

.Oh, dear! The sun of life has gone down. This body is leaving as it merges into the soil and turns into ashes. Memories become empty, and history disappears.

Oh, my dear...! The Goddess of Death...! I am coming...! What world are you in...? I am putting an end to this life, and I will reach you soon. Let us become one at least there. I am coming...!

Somebody kept a finger at the nose of the old man on the bed to see if he was breathing or not. Somebody held the hand and checked the pulse.

They tried to lift him by saying "Spread the mat... Lay the mattress..." Everyone crowded around and burst out weeping...

Sorrow filled the house.

Bathukamma, Namaste Telangana, Sunday Issue, 2016.

MONEY

"Hello! Namaskaram, Lecturer Saheb! I am Shekar. Are all of you well? Do you recognize me? How are the children and sister? I heard that your eldest has gone to the US."

. It took Rajesham some time to recognize the person behind that voice. Meanwhile, Shekar had been sharing some significant details from his end. In a short span of time, half an hour had passed.

Shekar paused and then continued, "You must find a way to help me out of this predicament."

"We had the intention to assist people by investing their funds in shares, engaging in real estate business, and multiplying their money through various avenues. However, we couldn't execute that plan," Shekar expressed. Rajesham chuckled softly at Shekar's words. They had presented alluring prizes and schemes to extract money from people's pockets, and now they were speaking as if they had performed a great service to the nation. "Perhaps this is how individuals adapt their beliefs over time," Rajesham contemplated.

Rajesham holds numerous memories within his mind. Shekhar is a distant relative of Rajesham. Rajesham is not a person who becomes entangled in anything.

Shekar earnestly requests, "Brother-in-law! Please do not forget. Your assistance is vital. I shall always remember your help in this lifetime."

In response, Lecturer Rajesham hums, saying, "Alright... I will certainly make an effort as much as possible."

Shekhar serves as the Chairman of Krishi Finance Limited, an organization that has amassed crores in deposits and stands as an exemplar for many. He achieved rapid financial growth within a short span, only to face an equally swift downfall. Currently, he is in hiding.

Following his graduation, Shaker initially undertook various odd jobs due to his inability to secure a postgraduate seat. He entered matrimony while managing a small hotel. Diligently saving the dowry funds, he purchased a piece of land located by the roadside, just outside the village. Fortune smiled upon him when a new bus stand was constructed nearby. He sold the land at a substantial price, which facilitated his venture into the plot business. With the expansion of his contacts, his business flourished.

He established a finance company with his friends, eventually becoming its chairman. He worked hard to increase the number of shareholders and depositors as the company grew through various stages. Over the course of ten years, the finance company gained a significant reputation and fame. They bought old buildings in Hyderabad, constructed apartments, and sold them. Dividends were distributed monthly, attracting new shareholders. This led to the establishment of new branches and subsidiaries. The companies, which had expanded to the extent of owning three cars and six crores, eventually collapsed before Rajesham's eyes, like a dream unravelling.

Now, in Shekhar's voice, the once-present pride and ego had disappeared. Rajesham recalled the times when Shekhar had been asked to help, and how many times Shekar asked him to see him. Interestingly, Rajesham found a certain contentment in Shekar being the one asking for his help this time. However, Rajesham was aware that there was little he could do to change the situation. Rajesham pondered the circumstances.

Shekhar had maintained cordial relationships with all parties, even if they didn't offer him support. He had spent considerable amounts on organizing star-studded nights featuring TV and film artists. All this began when he grew tired of being blackmailed by a political leader. He boldly told the leader to proceed with his intentions, which stirred discussions even in the Assembly. Shekhar explained that, emerging from a area of disadvantage, he had entered a competitive field, leading certain financial capitalists to provoke the government against him. Some attributed his troubles to changes in Reserve Bank policies. Rajesham, an Economics Lecturer, wondered why these entities were so fragile that a minor issue could cause their collapse. If the underlying problems were not concealed, why did crises erupt abruptly?

The financial capitalists, who had lined the pockets of officials from various government departments and a police officer, were forced to flee. Shekhar went into hiding because the people attacked his office, demanding the return of their deposits. They took whatever was available in the office and even manhandled him. Presently, his whereabouts are unknown – nobody knows where he is, what he's doing, or how he's living. There's no trace of him except for a few articles in the newspapers. After all these days, a phone call from Shekhar...

Where Shekhar's wife and children are now remains a question. What happened to their education? When asked about Rajeshwari's well-being, he sadly laughed and replied, "She asked me to get arrested and spend some time in jail. She can't handle the stress of not knowing what the future holds."

Unfortunately, as her husband's financial status grew, Rajeshwari distanced herself from both relatives and friends, looking down on them. She displayed an unwarranted pride, as if the car they owned had been acquired before her birth. Today, she finds herself without anyone to share her troubles with. In the end, she incessantly badgered her husband to go to jail, unable to endure the tension. Shekhar even refrained from returning home, suspecting that Rajeshwari might make a late-night phone call that could lead the police to him. Someone assured Rajeshwari that they wouldn't face any legal consequences.

"The notion of staying together during adversity may not seem sensible. If life becomes fractured, is it reasonable for life partners to each choose their own path?" thought Rajesham. His heart was filled with sadness.

"Brother-in-law," he said, "if you say they will surely agree. You just give the assurance. I can get out on bail from cases. Anyway, I have to surrender. I will file the IP. I can't talk like this when I went to jail. Sorry, brother-in-law. I didn't help you when I was in a good position. Many have received many favours from me, but now no one cares about me." His voice seemed to be hoarser with tears.

Rajesham's heart melted.

Lives that have grown step by step are greatly devastated in a short time. The share market is not in our hands. Who knows when and which share will rise and fall? Lakhs of shareholders lost thousands of crores due to the blow of Harshad Mehta. The share market suffered another blow from Ketan Parekh before recovering from it. With that, the share market across the country collapsed. How many went bankrupt?

"We don't know what happens after the money in our hands falls into their hands," Rajasham thought. He congratulated himself that he never got into such entanglements. He did not pay any deposits in any Finance Company no matter how much someone appealed for compliance in the name of kinship or friendship.

"Brother-in-law! Unemployed people like us will get some employment. We will give twenty thousand rupees for ten thousand after five years or pay twenty thousand as a shareholder, brother-in-law! We will pay four hundred for each share at the rate of two rupees interest per month. We will get an interest of three rupees, and we are paying interest at the rate of two rupees. We will all benefit," Shekhar asked him as he beseeched everyone. He evaded answering. But when his friends bought five shares and became directors of the finance company, and when they were drawing a monthly salary of one thousand rupees and cruising around in cars, he used to feel very disheartened. He was leading his life with an old Bajaj scooter. It was surprising to see the youngsters moving around in new cars and Hero Honda bikes in the name of finances. He had lost many relatives and friends because he did not invest in the finance. He still hadn't forgotten the experience of losing thousands of rupees when he paid towards chits in a chit fund company. So, he thought that he should never get into such matters. He had bought two plots of two hundred yards each at the rate of one hundred yards for two hundred rupees. Now they are worth fifty thousand rupees each due to these finances. He thought that was enough.

Rajesham returned to the present when Vishala asked him, "Do you have a holiday for your college today?"

"Who has been on the phone for such a long time?" asked Vishala casually.

Vishala explodes in anger if Sheker's name or Rajeshwari's name is mentioned. She asks others to stay away from them, given the extent of her negative experiences and humiliations involving them. After contemplating for a moment, Rajesham considers whether or not to disclose something and eventually breaks into a smile.

Rajesham decides against divulging into the matter and concludes, "Old friend, who hadn't been in touch for a while, called me today. He inquired about everyone and even remembered you. He also inquired about the city where our elder son is residing in the US."

Inquiring, Vishala asks, " The tiffin has gone cold. Should I reheat it?"

With that, he takes the towel and closes the bathroom door, stating, "Yes, please reheat it, and also prepare tea. I'm going to take a bath in the meantime."

As he enters the bathroom, a flood of memories rushes over him.

All those who used to travel around in cars have encountered financial ruin and are now living in secrecy without a known address. Depositors are now visiting residences, seeking ten thousand rupees, suggesting that receiving ten thousand rupees is preferable to not receiving twenty thousand rupees. The directors are making requests to settle at six thousand rupees for ten thousand rupees due to the company's financial losses. The Chairmen of Finance, CEOs, MDs, and CMDs are perpetuating this narrative through clandestine phone conversations with the directors yet keeping their own whereabouts undisclosed.

After heading directly to town from college, Rajesham meets his friends and converses about Shaker with some of them. They discuss potential courses of action. By the time he returns home, darkness has fallen, and the lights are already switched on.

Retrieving a visiting card from a niche, Vishala hands it over to Rajesham while saying, "A certain Ramamurthy, the manager at the Reserve Bank, came looking for you around 4 o'clock. He mentioned he's staying at Hotel Maneru in Karimnagar."

Surprisingly, Ramamurthy came from Hyderabad to Jagtial and arrived at his home, searching for himself.

Rajesham recalled an incident from two years ago, stating, "You should have asked him to have food."

Rajesham has a habit of inviting everyone who comes to his home to have food. "He didn't stop, even though I offered him tea. He arrived in a car. When I mentioned that you weren't home, he left as swiftly as he had come, mentioning that he would meet again," Vishala recounted.

Rajesham holds a great deal of respect for Ramamurthy, who is exceedingly unassuming and harmonizes with individuals, regardless of their stature.

Ramamurthy used to occasionally meet in conferences and literary gatherings.

After freshening up and having tea, Rajesham connected with Ramamurthy over the phone at the Karimnagar Maner Hotel.

Ramamurthy, after exchanging pleasantries, elaborated on the issue. "The Reserve Bank appointed me to an inquiry committee due to the substantial decline in bank deposits from your region over several years. A sum of 400 crores in deposits has diminished from your area, signifying that 400 crores have been amassed in the private sector, under the guise of financial institutions in your vicinity. These funds haven't been channelled into the production sector; instead, they're being diverted towards real estate, the stock market, and other ventures and lending the money to generate interest." Thus, Ramamurthy expounded on the policies of the Central Government, the Reserve Bank, and the State Governments.

From this, it can be inferred that all the confrontations with the police and the negative news surrounding Finance Companies in the newspapers were executed as part of a plan. Rajesham harbored suspicions that Marwadi and Gujarati investors were behind this plot, surmising that they orchestrated this scheme due to concerns that finance companies such as Shaker's, which had flourished with their investment of 400 crores, might pose a competitive threat to them. He shared his thoughts on this matter with Ramamurthy.

"Various rumours were spread," Rajesham argued, "How can a share of eleven rupees that rose to sixty rupees suddenly fall to three rupees? It is all a conspiracy. With that, all the depositors have asked to return their money at once. If everyone withdraws money at once, any bank will go bankrupt. How do the Finance Companies that are just settling survive?" "Half of the deposits have been allocated towards establishing the office, prize money, office furniture, cars, rents, and lands. Who is the sudden buyer of the land purchased for plotting? How can the money be returned to each individual?" Argued Rajesham.

"I don't agree with you," Ramamurthy responded. "If the deposits had been converted into investment in the industrial production sector or agriculture, the Finance Companies would not have become bankrupt, no matter how much the Reserve Bank, the Central and the State Governments harassed them. Investments were spent on pomp. Dead capital has increased. That is the real problem." Thus, Ramamurthy discussed the details of his commission of enquiry.

"Can't the government officials, police, big capitalists, Marwadi and Gujarati seths, share markets, and banks allow the local people to live on their own?" Rajesham asked pointedly. "The banks that collected deposits of eight hundred crores in our area are not giving at least two hundred crores of loans to the local people. Who should ask this? Are people there to raise your big banks and entrepreneurs?"

"What you said is true," Ramamurthy acknowledged. "Isn't it the industrialists who provide funds to the respective parties in the state and the centre? But no one can hinder those who grow up with discipline locally. Didn't Nirma powder company grow? Those who want to grow in shortcuts will collapse in that way."

Ramamurthy continued, "Why do people trust the share market along with figures like Harshad Mehta and Ketan Parekh? Why are people eagerly drawn to and buy shares? Don't the individuals have the right to engage in business together and carry on with their own pursuits while facing various pressures?"

Ramamurthy continued by discussing how the middle class is succumbing to a psychology of dependence. He delved into the reasons behind their involvement in various financial and chit fund scams, as well as their inclination to invest in the stock market in search of quick and easy money.

"Will you be there tomorrow?" asked Rajesham.

" I am leaving tonight," said Ramamurthy.

That night, Rajesham found it hard to sleep. He went through books about financial capital and kept thinking. 'In fact, what is money? How is money created? When the power of labor is the source of the relationship between the value of commodities and the value of gold, how can it fall into the hands of others in the form of money when all wealth arises from the power of labor itself? Paper currency has come into existence instead of gold and silver coins, lands, and properties. Had banks not emerged, the exchange of wealth would not have been so bad...!'

It is not known when he had fallen asleep.

He got up in the morning and continued his routine.

After fifteen days...

Shekhar went to jail as he didn't obtain bail. Following Shekhar's incarceration, all the burden shifted onto Rajeshwari. Rajeshwari couldn't fathom that this would transpire due to her husband's imprisonment. After the depositors obtained her address, they went to her residence in groups and subjected her to physical assault. Rajeshwari was overwhelmed by indescribable words, abuses, vulgar language, and curses.

Rajesham and others are putting in significant efforts with lawyers and police officers.

When someone seized Shekha's properties, there was an order from the court. A notice was posted, stating that distribution would be carried out by the court for those listed in the IP.

Rajeshwari, Shekhar's wife, couldn't endure the abuses, vulgar language, curses, and insults from the depositors. She was unsure about what to do. Eventually, she tragically ended her life by hanging herself.

Despite the attempts made by advocates and Rajesham to secure a one-day bail for Shekhar to view Rajeshwari's body before the cremation, they were unsuccessful.

. Upon learning of Rajeshwari's demise, Vishala was shattered. She went to pay her final respects.

"Bathukamma", Namaste Telangana, Sunday edition, 2016

LIBERATION FROM FREEDOM

Sahasra is not in the mood since Jaya called and told her decision after discussing it at length. Different kinds of thoughts are entering her mind. "How lives are taking turns!" she mused. "We think of one thing but something else happens! Without their involvement in this, why is there such a miserable condition in my life? Jaya has a very comfortable life and high respect in society. She has many staff members and is also earning. She has financial freedom as well. Yet, why does she have problems and difficulties?" Sahasra wondered.

If opinions don't align, is separation the only solution? When a husband does things, she doesn't like, is it proper to seek a divorce? If you can't live with those who have promised to share life's hardships and joys, if adjustment seems impossible, if change is beyond reach, how can one hope to adapt in the world? Does a life without compromise even exist? Can those who are unable to change their life partners truly expect to mould the world in their favour?

Amidst Sahasra's contemplations, the thought of her elder brother Manoj and Jaya, who once loved each other deeply but couldn't marry, crossed her mind. Might they hold novel perspectives now? Does Jaya revisit thoughts of her elder brother Manoj? If so, what will be the implications for sister-in-law Vishala? Sahasra's thoughts weave a complex tapestry, traversing diverse pathways. She concludes that she must discuss these musings with her father, patiently awaiting the opportune moment.

It's the rainy season, and the rain pours down like never before. Everywhere you look, there's lush greenery. The sky remains cloudy due to days of continuous rain, with heavy downpours adding to the spectacle.

Following the intense downpours, rivers and rivulets overflow, filling up the tanks that have been empty for so long. Despite the abundance of water, the rain keeps falling. Ponds and canals brim with water, leading to waterlogged roads. The overflowing water from the tank's spills over the surplus weir, bringing joy to children and adults who have been waiting for this moment.

With the water cascading over the weir, children and adults find happiness in this natural phenomenon. Children, in particular, are engrossed in play by the streams formed in front of their houses. They enthusiastically paper boats and let them sail in the flowing water. They also use iron rods in the soil to play, moving forward along the road. Covered in mud, they playfully mimic flying by spreading mud on their hands and feet. The muddy terrain leads cyclists to walk, carrying their bicycles, and even sandal-wearing individuals are walking while carrying their footwear.

The well-filled tanks are overflowing at the surplus weir, swiftly supplying water to the fields and ponds below. The rain steadily poured throughout the night, and by dawn, it transformed into floods. The water is still on the rise, overflowing the surplus weir, and causing the tanks' dams to break. Whenever a breach occurs in any of the tanks, all the water flows into the lower tank, resulting in the lower dams breaking as well. Cries for help echo in every village. Sandbags are being filled ceaselessly, and efforts are underway to prevent the tanks from rupturing. Grass and shrubs tumble into the streams and get carried away. Some trees, along with their roots, are swept away and fall along the stream banks.

A month has elapsed, and nature is now resplendent with greenery. Nature has once again stood tall following the disaster. People have put aside all memories of the calamity and have resumed their agricultural endeavours. Sahasra, along with her mother Madhavi and Principal Ramachandraiah, travelled together to a wedding function in a car and later returned.

The car runs smoothly on the road. The driver, who knows how to drive the car for Principal Ramachandraiah, is driving at a smooth speed. Ramachandraiah is happy to drive through the forest and hills to an old friend's function. The nature, surroundings, and journey in the car are very pleasant for Madhavi and Sahasra. With the trees on both sides of the road, fields, and hills in the distance, the hills are all green like a forest, and the chirping of birds in the sky makes Sahasra ecstatic to see the surroundings. She is saddened by how much she is missing in life in the busyness of work.

"Father! How captivating this nature is—the environment, the birds, the riverbank, and the dunes! How great it would be if a person could live freely immersed in these beauties of nature! What joy it would be to live in a cottage in such surroundings! Why do people run away from nature to towns and cities, Father? Is there truly freedom in towns and cities? It all seems like a running race. Is life in cities genuinely comfortable?" Lecturer Sahasra asked, as if she had suddenly remembered.

The river flows calmly from the left side. It feels like kissing the cold sand and forming sparrow nests. The clouds are moving across the sky like cotton. Sahasra has completely immersed herself in nature. They seem to be arriving from some grand wedding.

"There is a significant difference between staying here and merely enjoying the view from a distance like an audience. I am familiar with that difference. You cannot imagine the depth of that difference. Allow me to illustrate, for example: I will drop you off here from the car. Will you stay until evening, catch a bus, and return home sometime at night?" inquired her father, Ramachandraiah.

"My goodness! Alone! I'm afraid... Let all of us alight if we wish to," expressed Sahasra.

"Do you comprehend, Sahasra? You hold a profound affection for nature. Yet, what a formidable fear it is to reside alone amidst nature! It's intriguing how humans are apprehensive of their own freedom!" Principal Ramachandraiah chuckled.

Marriage, family, job responsibilities, and the like are also comparable. We desire liberation from them, yet we dread insecurity. We perceive them as safeguards, but at times, we lament their constrictions. Occasionally, we seek freedom within them. Freedom can be profoundly daunting for someone who cherishes liberty. Humans have harbored a love for freedom for millennia and have held a profound affinity for nature. However, following the industrial revolution and the establishment of modern democratic systems, humanity has grown distanced from nature. Contemporary humans adore nature, yet their attachment to society surpasses that sentiment. They believe that security, protection, employment, job opportunities, and comfort abide within society. This belief drives them to seek nature for recreation, making plans for holiday resorts and tours. Moreover, unlike our ancestors, present-day individuals are disinclined to coexist harmoniously with animals and birds by dwelling in nature. I surmise this is why the modern individual dreads genuine and unadulterated freedom. Ramchandraiah contemplated expressing that he thought Jiddu Krishnamurthy's perspective on freedom might be entirely accurate, but he hesitated, unsure whether he could fully endorse it or not.

Sahasra argued, saying, "I don't accept this statement, Father! Say whatever you want... Man loves freedom, Father! He gives up everything for freedom."

" Sahasra...! Freedom is relative. Freedom is defined as a part of society. Manu, while stating in Manusmriti, mentioned that a woman's trajectory should be, in childhood, with parents; in youth, with her husband; in old age, with her children. He stated, "Nasthri swathanthryamarhathi," implying that women do not deserve freedom. It appears that the author of Manusmriti believed and expressed this view, observing that a woman's roles as a mother and a wife are vital for the stability of the family system. According to this perspective, if a woman becomes independent, the foundations of the family system would be shaken, leading to the dissolution of the family structure."

"Father, you are right. No matter how much you talk about women's equality, the right to vote, and gender parity, where is the actual freedom for women? You curtailed the freedom we had in childhood in the name of discipline. Despite Manoj, the elder brother, desiring to love and marry Jaya, you colluded with Jaya's father, uncle Bhaskar, to prevent their marriage. You have no idea how much she is suffering now. Dad, indeed, where is the freedom for women these days, especially after marriage? I don't mean to say that your son-in-law Sudhakar is bad. He is relatively good compared to Jaya's husband. Nevertheless, women have minimal freedom within this marriage system. I want to pursue a job. He is engrossed in his role as an RDO (Revenue Divisional Officer). Both of us are always occupied. Where is the freedom in this scenario? Life is progressing along its predefined path, much like a train journey....," expressed Sahasra.

"Where is freedom for me? I lost my freedom when I got married. The goal of your mother and me is to live in harmony with each other. Thus, your mother and I got deliverance from freedom as soon as we got married. We sacrificed personal freedom by compromising and understanding each other. I had to live all my life for you and your mother. After marriage, it is the same for everyone. Where is the individual freedom left for me and your mother? Your mother gave up her freedom for the well-being of us all. Thus, after marriage, after the formation of a family, and after having children, we devoted ourselves to the family. As a result, we both became free from liberty. And so have you. Does your husband have the freedom? You say your husband is your property..."

"Mother also protects you like her property and threatens you....!" laughed Sahasra.

Mother Madhavi still wants to listen to that discussion.

Madhavi burst out with her anguish, saying, "Where do I have freedom? When I was a child, my parents, after marriage your father, and then you... All were the ones who restricted me. My whole life is spent serving you all."

As the father explains freedom in its various aspects, daughter Sahasra asks to know more.

"So, Sahasra! Your mother cannot tolerate freedom. Women like you also cannot tolerate freedom...! By being dependent, they seek happiness, security, and comfort," said Ramachandraiah.

"That is your old-fashioned Ness, Dad! I love freedom very much. I am not like Mom," said Sahasra. She was overwhelmed with anger.

"So, can you tell me why you got married?" Ramchandraiah asked point-blank with a smile.

Mother Madhavi interfered and said angrily, 'How can you say that? For a woman, marriage is like a stake for tethering. No matter how much you turn around, you have to go around it only.'"

"Why do you think that way, Mom? Shouldn't a woman get a divorce when she has to live a life she doesn't like?" Lecturer Sahasra inquired.

"How would you have managed if we had divorced? It was tough to lose your father's love and for me to support you alone," Mother Madhavi explained.

."Mom, that's your problem. Nowadays, many people like me are living independently. They have jobs like men. They handle household chores and raise children as well."

"Jaya wants to get a divorce. It is said that her husband is wandering around making films; he is going somewhere with someone else; he's not coming home... Jaya's thoughts might have turned to elder brother Manoj," Mother Madhavi said as she attempted to meet her father's gaze.

Madhavi was shocked, as if a bomb had fallen by her side. Ramachandraiah, who had been lost in a meditative sleep in the car, suddenly opened his eyes.

"Has Jaya gone crazy? Why is she thinking in such a way?" exclaimed Madhavi.

"Mom! Jaya feels the same way you do about the lack of freedom in your whole life. But it's not just about good and bad, Mom! Jaya longs for freedom. She wants to live as a single parent with her children! Is there any fault in her thinking? She has gained some experience of marriage, family, and children. She had some illusions before marriage, some hopes. People think they will achieve something. Nobody truly has freedom within this family system, Dad!" Lecturer Sahasra passionately expressed.

"Sahasra! Can Jaya achieve freedom through divorce? Is it genuine freedom? Pre-marriage freedom differs from post-divorce freedom. These two situations are not the same. Does Jaya comprehend this?" Ramachandraiah inquired.

Madhavi expressed surprise, saying, "Are you suggesting that Jaya is getting a divorce? Turning to Sahasra, she asked, "What exactly happened?"

"It's been rumoured that she's become disillusioned with her family," Sahasra evasively replied without revealing the complete truth.

"Sahasra! Right after getting married and having children for some time, that is, after ten years of marriage, I also felt that I should run away from this marriage, family, bonds, and the race of life. I yearned for freedom. A friend of mine left his wife and children for the sake of society. Another friend went to the Himalayas in pursuit of freedom, spiritual growth, and meditation. After a while, nobody knew what occurred, but both returned to their families. However, their families were already torn apart. Their attitudes had changed. Family members consistently quarreled with and tormented them, saying, 'You are not living for us; you have come for yourself; you don't love us, and if you truly loved us, you wouldn't have abandoned us in misery.'"

Regardless of their actions, their sacrifices and contributions went unnoticed. They relinquished their freedom, ambitions, and dreams, either making compromises or dedicating their entire lives to their families. They made numerous sacrifices to ensure their children could receive a good education and prosper. They succeeded in their endeavours, even relocating to countries like the UK, the US, Canada, Australia, Germany, and New Zealand, and establishing themselves there. Nevertheless, they still face criticism from their children. Forgiveness eludes them. They yearn for family harmony. It remains unclear why, but they once again became the family's mainstay. Nevertheless, neither the wife nor the children could bring themselves to forgive them.

"Dad, I'm having trouble understanding your perspective. On one hand, you remind me that Mother didn't get to live freely. But on the other hand, when Jaya wants to get a divorce, you question whether that's considered freedom," Sahasra voiced her confusion, inundating her father with a barrage of questions.

Principal Ramachandraiah contemplated the potential outcomes of Jaya's separation from various angles. He recognized that both Jaya and Sahasra were no longer children. Instead of maintaining an authoritarian demeanour as he had before, he believed it was crucial to communicate and elaborate on different aspects.

"Sahasra, consider this: if Jaya raises her children as a single parent without their father, will her children forgive her in the future? Think about it. Even if Jaya remarries or reconciles with her husband down the line, will her children and husband truly acknowledge and pardon her, regardless of the sacrifices she's made and the services she's rendered? Ponder over this... Pre-marriage freedom differs from the freedom of leaving a family after marriage or obtaining a divorce. These two scenarios aren't equivalent. Sure, anyone can choose to live freely without marriage, opting for a celibate life. But you've observed the lives of our acquaintances and witnessed how society treats their children when they seek such liberation after marriage or when Jaya departs from the family! You're well aware of the individuals I'm referring to."

"Madhavi comprehends the situation with those acquaintances all too well. She's also familiar with the harassment their wives subject them to. Madhavi finds it puzzling, whenever she recalls them, why they've transformed into such individuals, continuously tormenting themselves and fixating on the past. Despite numerous explanations and advice, their inherent nature remains unaltered. Despite receiving everything from Dad, they persistently make life miserable for him."

Madhavi and Sahasra are well acquainted with these matters. Ramachandraiah paused for a moment and then resumed speaking.

"Even now, they don't make phone calls to converse; they share everything with their mother. Fathers are considered outsiders to those families. Their father's role never factors into their considerations. However, without their father's involvement, there can be no development. Why does this paradox exist? It is often said that as a man matures, he develops his personality, nature, and culture. But regardless of their growth, why do they behave in this manner towards their past, memories, and father? Can we expect Jaya to desire such a life? Can we assume that even though Jaya entrusted her children to her husband, her children will not harbour resentment towards either Jaya or their father as they grow older? Won't they consistently criticize Jaya, claiming they were deprived of parental love and faced numerous societal insults? Is Jaya prepared to confront this? Can Jaya experience true freedom even if her children criticize and despise her to the extent that she feels she must nurture them?" Ramachandraiah looked back at his daughter for her opinion.

The car was moving swiftly but decelerated suddenly with a jolt.

Sahasra contemplated deeply. It's unclear whether her father is advocating for Jaya's divorce or not. It would have been more helpful if he had provided some clarity.

Man is not an independent being rather, he is a social creature. While living in society, man craves freedom. Furthermore, man cannot exist autonomously in nature. Some individuals willingly embrace the bonds and associations of communal life. Does every attachment signify an escape from freedom? What defines freedom? Can a bird soaring in the sky be considered genuinely free? Is its flight a representation of freedom? Is its search for sustenance an illustration of freedom? Or is freedom synonymous with inevitability? Can freedom be defined as breaking free from the grasp of inevitability?

Ramachandraiah urged her to delve deeper into her thoughts, stating, "During my childhood, I fled to my aunt's house, driven by the fear of my father's reprimands. From my perspective, it was a departure from confinement towards liberation. However, from my parents' perspective, it was an evasion of discipline."

Father-daughter talks have shifted from topic to topic.

Is the river a symbol of freedom?

Does the river possess freedom?

A mother is a river.

A woman is a river.

Does a mother have the freedom?

"Do you consider living in nature, detached from reactions and actions, as freedom?"

Is it accurate to believe that nature doesn't react to actions while existing in freedom?

Man aspires to grow like a tree, yet desires to twirl like a creeper.

Feminists label being a wife and a mother as indicative of dependent psychology. This is a reality.

But why do they live in dependency? Is it solely due to a lack of financial freedom?

Is it purely because of a deficiency in the freedom of decision-making?

Ponder upon this at least once.

Has the mother lost her freedom? Has she found salvation through freedom?

Women revolt when they yearn for freedom.

When we envision freedom as the liberty of self-determination, isn't it a facet of selfishness?

Living in a state devoid of desires signifies genuine freedom. If you seek to live freely, you must shed selfishness. Liberation from freedom implies liberation from selfishness.

Is the freedom of subjective thinking equivalent to the freedom linked to self-mental inclination?

Ramachandraiah posed numerous questions, asking, "Is true freedom achievable only when one breaks free from the ties of worldly life, from all physical and emotional attachments, and even blood relations? Is it feasible?" Sahasra was engulfed in that sequence of questions. Each question pierced like an arrow.

It's stated that freedom equates to Samadhi. What is Samadhi? It's said that Samadhi is existing in a state beyond attachment to the bonds of mundane life!

"Sahasra! For whom, the state of Samadhi is meant for? Why is it so? Is it for self-happiness? If self-satisfaction is paramount, what is the relationship between it and society? What do those practicing it have to do with society? And what does society have to do with them? Why should society care about them? Why should it contemplate these matters?"

Sahasra, at her age, didn't grasp those questions fully. Ramachandraiah didn't seem to notice as he continued speaking.

Freedom in a relationship... Freedom in attachment... Freedom in captivity... Freedom in employment... Freedom in marriage... Freedom in family... Freedom in a voluntarily and selflessly lived life is true freedom.

How can mere self-enjoyment be considered selfless enjoyment? These questions felt like thrusting a spear into the ego.

Is it selfish for a person to grow freely without any hindrances, nurturing their creativity, uniqueness, and specialty, and to pursue them? Is it solely for self-pleasure? Sahasra couldn't bear those words.

Sahasra voiced her protest, saying, "What you're describing is thought policing."

Ramachandraiah burst into laughter.

"Sahasra! Administration means guiding thought processes. To be precise, it's essentially thought policing. Administration, discipline, and administrative management are like the two opposite banks of a river. The state, constitution, democratic system, social system, monarchy, industrial system, family system, and so on, all influence and shape the thoughts of society's members as they deem appropriate. If you resist, they will impose constraints on you. At times, people rebel against this imposition and gain additional rights. Yet again, they must coexist within their respective systems.

"Thus, a headmaster means a big head. What do teachers do? They change their mindset. Or they set the mindset. The respective societies create these orientations based on their place and time."

."Dad! So, as a social being, does man continue to experience some form of thought policing and control over certain physical and emotional bonds throughout his life?"

"Now, do you understand the point? Mom found redemption from these mundane bonds and lives freely. She has relinquished selfishness within that freedom. Hence, your mother attained deliverance from selfish freedom."

"Deliverance from freedom implies deliverance from selfishness. It signifies selfless freedom liberated from selfishness and self-indulgence. This freedom is both universal and enduring. Similarly, the concept of deliverance from freedom is synonymous with freedom from excessive selfishness and self-centeredness."

"Freedom, freed from selfishness, embraces humanity and nature with love."

"When liberated from egocentric personal freedom, a person develops love for others and humanity."

"Universal love extends to nature and humanity. Selfless love and universal freedom share the same level of significance. In essence, practicing unconditional love does not equate to true freedom."

."If Jaya desires to live freely, that is her prerogative. While she faces challenges, let us continue supporting her and her parents."

"If Jaya seeks deliverance from freedom, does she require a divorce?" Ramchandraiah refrained from speaking.

"A moment of silence filled the car. Was Madhavi performing all her roles as a wife and mother as a means of liberation from freedom? Perhaps that's why she diligently attended to the family's needs and children's comforts all these years. Madhavi appeared to have uncovered something new."

."Does individual freedom symbolize selfishness? Is the inability to engage in mutual attachments with a life partner a genuine manifestation of freedom? Can it be seen as selfishness? Is it possible for those who struggle to form a partnership in life to build connections with others and coexist within society? Does this constitute a self-centered life?"

"Sahasra! Where would all of you be if I desired freedom? How did your father live? How did your brothers live? Reflect upon what your lives would have turned into," cautioned Mother Madhavi.

Sahasra grew solemn. Is there nothing but selfishness in the freedom that everyone talks about?

Can the growth of freedom in a person occur creatively without any hindrances? Is striving not only for one's own freedom, but also for the freedom of others, true freedom? Is this the essence of motherhood? Is this the contentment that Father experienced as the head of the family?

The car is progressing along the road.

Diverse thoughts were circulating among the four individuals, including the driver.

Liberation from freedom implies liberation from selfishness. It involves gaining freedom from the clutches of selfishness and desires. True freedom involves conquering desires. Converting desires into goals is inherently selfish. Buddha proclaimed that desires are the root of sorrow. This signifies that selfishness is the source of sorrow. How can one exist without any desires? Isn't altruism a form of desire? The struggle for survival isn't synonymous with selfishness. In one of his ghazals, C. Narayana Reddy contemplates, "What kind of life does a person have if not lived for others' sake?" Does feminism equate to selfishness? Existential and feminist movements do not arise from selfish motives... They are aimed at empowerment...! Isn't feminism, existential movements, and all such endeavours philanthropic to the extent that they collectively strive for the greater good of all? It becomes selfish if they solely serve one's own interests. Sahasra pondered these questions. She voiced the same inquiry.

Principal Ramachandraiah said, persuading and explaining to her daughter, "Yes... Now you know the truth. The idea of freedom without cooperation, mutual sacrifice, and mutual love is not at all pure selfishness."

Is self-determined freedom another name for selfishness? Is there only selfishness in Jaya's idea of divorce? Is it self-determined freedom? Is brother Manoj in touch with Jaya over the phone? What does Jaya actually think about her future? Is there only selfishness in her thinking of living in Nagpur as a single parent, doing her own work and living away from everyone? How does she overcome the sense of inferiority that affects the children? Will the problem be resolved over time by living apart without getting a divorce...?

Sahasra was shocked by her parents' words. Do we need to consider the other side of freedom? Negotiation and persuasion are necessary for Jaya. Sahasra thought of telling Jaya that there is no better life outside the family, which one can enjoy as a single parent.

Nature greets them with chilliness, greenery, and lustre.

Sahasra's thoughts are moving in different directions. She is losing the ability to enjoy the pleasures that nature and the surroundings offer. Sahasra is experiencing an intractable conflict.

New Desires (Modern Short Stories)

KASTURI VIJAYAM

📞 00-91 95150 54998
KASTURIVIJAYAM@GMAIL.COM

SUPPORTS

- **PUBLISH YOUR BOOK AS YOUR OWN PUBLISHER.**

- **PAPERBACK & E-BOOK SELF-PUBLISHING**

- **SUPPORT PRINT ON-DEMAND.**

- **YOUR PRINTED BOOKS AVAILABLE AROUND THE WORLD.**

- **EASY TO MANAGE YOUR BOOK'S LOGISTICS AND TRACK YOUR REPORTING.**